CREAM BUNS AND CRIME

Also by Robin Stevens:

MURDER MOST UNLADYLIKE
ARSENIC FOR TEA
FIRST CLASS MURDER
JOLLY FOUL PLAY
MISTLETOE AND MURDER

Coming soon:
THE GUGGENHEIM MYSTERY

A sequel to the award-winning *The London Eye Mystery*

by Siobhan Dowd

Cream Buns AND CRIME

A MURDER
MOST UNLADYLIKE
Collection

ROBIN STEVENS

PUFFIN

PUFFIN BOOKS

UK | USA | Canada | Ireland | Australia
India | New Zealand | South Africa

Puffin Books is part of the Penguin Random House group of companies
whose addresses can be found at global.penguinrandomhouse.com.

www.penguin.co.uk
www.puffin.co.uk
www.ladybird.co.uk

Penguin
Random House
UK

First published 2017

009

Text copyright © Robin Stevens, 2017
Cover and illustrations copyright © Nina Tara, 2017
Additional illustrations copyright © Shutterstock, 2017

Every effort has been made to trace copyright holders.
The publisher would like to hear from any copyright holder not acknowledged.

The moral right of the author and illustrator has been asserted

Set in 11/16 pt ITC New Baskerville
Typeset by Jouve (UK), Milton Keynes

Printed and bound in Great Britain by Clays Ltd, Elcograf S.p.A.

A CIP catalogue record for this book is available from the British Library

ISBN: 978–0–141–37656–1

All correspondence to:
Puffin Books
Penguin Random House Children's
80 Strand, London WC2R 0RL

To all my Detective Society members, everywhere.

CREAM BUNS AND CRIME

Being an account of cases old and new
from the Detective Society and the
Junior Pinkertons.

Featuring tips, tales, recipes and detective secrets.

January 1936

CONTENTS

How to set up your own detective society

Hello, aspiring detectives! Daisy Wells here. Hazel and I have agreed that readers of this book ought to know how to put a Detective Society together, so that they can prepare themselves to counter criminal activity. We have decided to explain our methods here. Please note that Hazel and I have rather different ideas when it comes to setting up a Detective Society. Mine are better, because I am an excellent Detective Society President, but you might as well have Hazel's too.

So here are the crucial steps you need to follow to create your very own Detective Society. Find a notebook to use as a casebook, pick up a squashed fly biscuit (if you have good taste like me) or a chocolate bourbon (if you are more like Hazel), and we can begin.

1. Choose your members

I would advise you to keep your Society to two members, if possible. This way, you won't have anyone interfering or giving away Society secrets.

Hazel, on the other hand, thinks that additional members *should* be allowed, provided they are people you can trust. She believes that working together is the better option, because you can share clues and information and so cover more ground. I am not so sure, although I admit there is *some* truth in what she says. Our own assistant members (our dorm mates, Kitty, Lavinia and Beanie) have been quite resourceful at times. But remember, your Society must be extremely careful when selecting its members. Make sure that every member promises to keep the Society a secret, to diligently look for clues, and to do everything it takes to pursue truth and justice!

2. Choose your Detective Society's name

Every good society needs an excellent detective name. Hazel and I chose the Wells and Wong Detective Society, and Alexander and George (our greatest rivals) chose the Junior Pinkertons. Those names are taken now, so you will have to come up with something different but just as brilliant. It helps if you have names that sound nice together, the way Hazel and I do, but even if you don't, think about words that are to do with detection or criminal activity and you'll have a serviceable Society name in no time!

3. Give out detective roles

First, and most importantly, you will need a President. The President runs the Society, makes all the most important decisions, and catches the criminal at the end of each case. It is the most important and responsible role by far. It is also the most glamorous.

You must also make sure you have a Vice-President and a Secretary. This can be the same person, as in our Society, or (if you insist on letting more people in) different ones.

The Vice-President's main job is to support the President in everything they do and say. The Vice-President is the Watson to the President's Sherlock, the Hastings to their Poirot. They may occasionally have ideas and opinions themselves – though the President shouldn't allow this too often.

It is the Secretary's job to write up all the Society's case notes in a neat and methodical manner. Do make sure that you pick someone with decent handwriting. Hazel's handwriting is very nice when she is not using shorthand.

All other members should begin as assistants, and rise up the ranks if they are good at their jobs. Assign each assistant a task, and remember to let people play to their strengths. For instance, Lavinia is not afraid to get her hands dirty. This is alarming, but it can also be useful. Kitty, because she loves gossip, is a great *noticer* of things, and Beanie . . . well, Beanie is wonderfully small, which means she is often overlooked, and can therefore observe suspects without being noticed herself.

4. Make your pledge

Once you have found members you can trust and decided on everyone's role, the next step is for everyone to take the Society's pledge.

Your pledge is a sort of promise. You are vowing to use all your skills to find clues and evidence, to report any observations to your superior members and, most importantly, to keep all detective business a secret! No one wants any grown-ups involved (unless they absolutely have to be).

If you don't want to think up your own pledge, I have decided to allow you to use ours. This is very kind of me, and you ought to thank me.

Do you swear to be a good and clever member of the Detective Society, and to logically detect the crimes presented to you using all the cleverness you have, not placing reliance on grown-ups, especially the police? Do you solemnly swear never to conceal a vital clue from your Detective Society President and Vice-President, and to do exactly what they say? Do you promise never to mention this to another soul, living or dead, on pain of medieval tortures?

At this point, each member must say *I do.* Then it is official.

5. Create a secret handshake

Every Society needs a secret handshake. Ensure yours is as complicated and devious as possible, and practise it regularly.

6. Decide on a time and place for meetings

Next you must think up a time and a place to hold your meetings.

The best meeting locations, in my experience, are empty dorm rooms (ordinary bedrooms will also do), locked bathrooms (with the water running to mask the sound of your voices) or small cupboards such as linen closets, but anywhere secluded but safe works very well. Make sure your Secretary has light and space for note-taking.

Meetings should be held regularly, and they become especially important when you are on a case. Remember that occasionally you may need to call an emergency meeting – for example, if a crucial piece of evidence comes to light in your latest case. Middle-of-the-night meetings are by far the most exciting. Invite your friends to your house, if you are not lucky enough to go to boarding school, and then hold a midnight feast!

7. Keep a casebook

This is one of the things that the Secretary does. I don't really bother about it, but as I discovered during the Bonfire Night Murder Case, it is rather important. *Not* taking notes will leave any detective, no matter how brilliant, in a dreadful muddle. I am now rather grudgingly impressed with Hazel, who is rigorous about recording everything in her casebook.

It is essential that a decent written record is kept of all the meetings that take place, and of any developments in the case. If something were to be missed, a crucial piece of evidence might be lost, and the pieces of the puzzle would never fit together.

Hazel is also very clever at compiling a suspect list for every case we investigate. Doing this in a sensible, logical way, and crossing off suspects once we have ruled them out, is very important in our hunt for the true culprit.

8. Get your kit together

A Detective Society should always have the right tools for the job. This should include a fingerprint kit (if you can't get hold of a proper professional one, make your own – we will explain how later in this book), a reliable wristwatch, some string or measuring tape for analysing suspicious objects, and a selection of disguises such as wigs, hats and old clothes.

A magnifying glass is perhaps the most crucial item, and no detective should ever be without one. I keep a miniature version on my person at all times.

Finally Hazel has asked me to add that a ready supply of pencils and a notebook should be carried by your Secretary, while tea and cakes will keep your detectives' strength up. No one can detect on an empty stomach, and as you know, the Detective Society never says no to tea.

9. Establish a rivalry with another society

Hazel thinks that working with another team of detectives can help you solve your case. I couldn't disagree more. At best, you are at risk of sharing your glory; at worst, you may find that your rivals reveal your secrets and ruin your case. Of course, Alex and George *were* occasionally useful to us during our Cambridge case, but I feel sure we would have solved it on our own anyway. My advice is to find another group of detectives and take every opportunity to pit your wits against them. It is most important to discover which is the best Society!

10. Constant vigilance!

Lastly Hazel would like me to point out that the best detectives stay safe. This is another way of saying that a dead detective is a very useless detective indeed. It is most important that you do not put yourself in *too* much danger while you are investigating your cases. Make sure that your hiding places and footholds are secure, that your suspects do not notice your presence and that you always alert the other members of your Society as to where you are and what you are doing.

Good luck, Detectives, and may you solve every case!

The Case of Lavinia's Missing Tie

Being an account of

The Wells and Wong Detective Society's First Case.

Written by Hazel Wong
(Detective Society Vice-President and Secretary),
aged 14.

Begun Tuesday 18th September 1934.

Here is something funny that I found in our Society's case files recently: the first-ever case the Detective Society solved! This case was from before we were murder detectives, before Miss Bell and Mr Curtis and all the other things that have happened to us. It seems dreadfully far away now, and for all that we thought we were grown-up, we were practically shrimps.

I almost didn't want to show it in this book, but Daisy says that it was all good practice for us, and anyway, all criminals, even tie thieves, have done wrong and need to be brought to justice.

You ought to note, too, that this case was investigated before Lavinia, Kitty and Beanie had been admitted to the Detective Society. It was still a secret from them, and from everyone!

— Hazel Wong

I

Tuesday 18th
September 1934

Lavinia came down to breakfast this morning five minutes late, and looking extremely cross. She thumped down in her seat, dark hair sticking up in a mop so stiff that I wondered whether the brush was still buried inside it. She snatched a piece of toast from the rack quite rudely, just as Sophie Croke-Finchley from the other dorm was reaching for it, and drew the butter dish towards her with a horrible clatter.

'Rude!' cried Sophie. 'I was going to take that!'

'Bother the butter,' said Lavinia. 'Someone's taken my tie. My *tie*!'

Lavinia is much given to fibbing – and is also fearfully disorganized – so we all looked at each other disbelievingly.

'Nonsense,' said Kitty. 'And anyway, haven't you any others?'

'One fell into my ink-pot last week and the other's ripped,' growled Lavinia.

'Oh dear, how did you rip it?' asked Beanie.

'I bit it,' said Lavinia. 'I couldn't make my sums add up properly.'

'Oh,' said Beanie. 'You can borrow my spare one.'

'No, she *can't*,' said Kitty. 'Lavinia, I bet it's under your bed, or in your games kit, or something.'

'Well, it isn't,' said Lavinia. 'Because the last time I saw it was last night, when it was hanging over the foot of my bed. I didn't move it, and it didn't walk away on its own, did it? So someone must have stolen it. Do you think I'm stupid?'

'Yes,' said Kitty.

'No,' said Beanie at the same time.

Clementine, who is in the other dorm with Sophie, snickered quite cruelly at that, and Lavinia glared at her.

'You wouldn't be laughing if it was your tie,' she said.

'Well, it isn't,' said Clementine. 'Anyway, you've just mislaid it, I'll bet you anything. Oh, *won't* you get it from Matron!'

'I haven't!' cried Lavinia. 'I *haven't*! Why won't any of you believe me?'

'Because you're a *liar*, Lavinia Temple,' said Clementine. 'You lied about your family, and now you're lying about this.'

'DON'T YOU DARE TALK ABOUT MY FAMILY!' roared Lavinia, and she launched herself at Clementine, knocking Beanie sideways.

We all jumped on Lavinia – we are used to dealing with her tantrums by now – and the prefect on duty at the third-form table leaped up and shouted for Matron. Lavinia was led away, still raging, and the loss of her tie became the least of her worries.

But Daisy nudged me and winked, and I knew that meant one thing: the Detective Society had its first case.

II

We interviewed Lavinia at lunch time. Beanie had discovered that she couldn't find her spare tie after all, and so Daisy had donated hers – which I think may have been a clever ploy on Daisy's part. Lavinia, as far as she could, seemed grateful.

'Thanks, I suppose,' she said. 'I still want my tie, though. I know one of you took it.'

'It wasn't *me*,' said Daisy. 'And it wasn't Hazel. Hazel, tell her.'

I shook my head, and then nodded, and then felt confused. 'It *wasn't* me,' I said. 'Really.'

'You know you can trust us,' said Daisy silkily. 'So, what happened? Tell us everything. Hazel, write it down.'

'I went to sleep. It was there. I woke up. It was gone,' said Lavinia, who was not turning out to be a natural witness.

'And where *was* it, when it was there?' asked Daisy, rolling her eyes. 'You have to tell us where it disappeared from, otherwise we'll never be able to get it back to you.'

'It was on the end of my bed, *obviously*. Where else would it be? You've seen me put it there, Daisy. Are you trying to be stupid?'

Daisy opened her mouth and then shut it again. I could tell she had been about to say something cutting about the Detective Society, but caught herself in time. The Detective Society is deadly secret, and no one knows that more than Daisy – she would never have forgiven herself if she had let information slip to Lavinia, who could be quite cruel when she wanted to, and who could never be trusted with anything important as a result.

'She just wanted to be sure,' I put in.

'So? Doesn't excuse asking idiotic questions. You all saw me take it off when we put on pyjamas last night. I don't know what happened after that, but *I* didn't move it.'

That was all we could get out of her. The rest of the dorm were not much more helpful.

'I didn't see it,' said Beanie, coming into the common room with Kitty. 'And I didn't take it, honestly I didn't. Poor Lavinia!'

'No one thinks you took it, Beanie,' said Kitty. 'And *poor Lavinia* nothing! She's been a beast this term.

16

Remember her punching Clementine during lacrosse? And just because Clementine said she came from a broken home, which is perfectly true. Honestly, that business with her father was *last year*. She ought to be over it by now.'

'Yes, of course she ought,' said Daisy. 'Hazel, come with me. We've got things to do.'

III

'Now, Watson,' said Daisy, sitting down with a bounce on her bed. 'I hereby call this meeting of the Detective Society to discuss the Case of Lavinia's Missing Tie to order. Present are Daisy Wells (which is me), President of the Detective Society, and Hazel Wong (which is you), Secretary. Have you written that down?'

I nodded.

'All right. Now, the facts in the case. What do we know?'

'Lavinia's tie was on the end of her bed on Monday evening, when she took it off,' I said. 'And on Tuesday morning it was gone.'

'Exactly,' said Daisy. 'Now, as we must admit, Lavinia is a liar. But in this case I happen to be able to confirm that she is telling the truth, at least about taking off the tie and hanging it on her bed. I saw it there as we came back from toothbrushes. Lavinia's bed is just by the door, after all. Last night Beanie knocked into me, and I tripped and banged my shin on the bed frame – and the tie was there then; I recall it distinctly. So someone must have moved it. But who, and how?'

'Could Lavinia have done it?' I asked.

'To blame someone else, you mean? But she isn't blaming anyone in particular, is she? She's just saying that it's gone. And anyway, Lavinia simply isn't very intelligent. She'd never come up with a plan like that. No, Watson, we must think of another solution. Let's see. We didn't do it, that's obvious. Beanie didn't do it – if she had, she'd have confessed in an instant. She's too nice for pranks. Kitty, now – *she* might play that sort of prank. She as good as told us earlier that she's cross with Lavinia for being so unpleasant this term. She might have decided to teach her a lesson. What do you think?'

'Um,' I said. 'But Kitty *likes* Lavinia, even if they do annoy each other.'

'So? Oh, all right then, let's think of some other suspects.'

'What if Matron took it to mend?'

'Last thing at night? When has she ever been so conscientious as to stay up darning? And anyway, *that* tie wasn't the ripped one. Lavinia said so. It was one of her *other* ties that was ripped. Think now, Hazel. What did you observe? Was anything out of the ordinary?'

I thought back to last night. We had come back from toothbrushes, Daisy bumping against Lavinia's bed on the way. We had climbed into bed, and the prefect on duty had clicked off the light and closed the door. I had shut my eyes and fallen asleep. It was the most ordinary bedtime imaginable.

I had even dreamed of dull things. In my sleep, we had climbed into bed, and the prefect on duty had closed the door, shutting off the light falling on Lavinia's bed from the corridor outside. *Again*, I dream-thought. *What a bore.*

It had been so detailed too, just like all the most ordinary dreams. Just as though – I sat up on Daisy's bed – just as though it had *really happened*.

'Daisy!' I cried. 'Daisy, I've remembered something! *The door closed twice!*'

IV

'So,' hissed Daisy as we filed into Science, 'we must hunt for our thief *outside* our dorm; someone who would have had to open the door to get at the tie. And the most likely place to find her is *the rest of the third form*! No one in the other dorm likes Lavinia at all. But which of them was it? Wait, don't reply now. The Bell's on the warpath again. We'll discuss after school.'

I shut my lips and nodded. She was quite right. Our Science mistress, Miss Bell, was looking coldly furious, and I could tell that the smallest bit of disobedience would get the culprit Detention at once. Poor Miss Bell. She has good reason to be so cross – our new Music and Art master, Mr Reid, who she seemed to be so friendly with at the beginning of term, has just thrown her over for Miss Hopkins, our Games mistress. It is very shocking, and everyone is holding their breath to see what will happen next. But during the lesson, as Miss Bell scratched away at the chalkboard and got dust all over her immaculate white lab coat, I closed my ears and let my mind drift off to the mystery.

And as soon as I thought about it properly, I saw that there could only really be one answer. Which girl in the other dorm had the most reason to hate Lavinia and would want to punish her with a prank? Clementine, of course. We had all seen Lavinia hit her in Games the week before, and Clementine is not one to let a slight like that go without getting her revenge. I had to tell Daisy – and as soon as we were out of the Science lab door, I turned to her to speak.

'I know who it was,' whispered Daisy. '*It was Clementine.*'

It is very difficult having a Detective Society with Daisy sometimes. Every time I think I've thought of something really clever, she turns out to have thought of it first. At least I know that she deserves to be President.

'I think so too!' I hissed back, looking over nervously as Clementine rushed past, shouldering her school bag and tying back her hair as she chattered to Sophie Croke-Finchley. 'But how do we prove it was her? Everyone in her dorm will just stick up for her!'

'Not necessarily,' said Daisy. 'You always believe people are too nice, Hazel, that's the problem with you. Half of that dorm are fearfully jealous of her – they'll crack if we give them the slightest opportunity. But that's all irrelevant. I don't mean to get one of the others to give her up. I want Clementine to confess herself.'

'But *how*?' I cried.

'By setting a trap for her, of course,' said Daisy.

V

'Have you heard?' said Daisy to Kitty and Beanie on the way up to House that evening. 'Clementine's been *sleepwalking*.'

'No!' said Kitty, who can always be relied on to spread gossip. '*Really*?'

'Oh yes,' said Daisy. 'It's true. Lots of people have seen her at it. Why, I heard Belinda Vance saying to Virginia Overton only last night that she'd seen

Clementine wandering the corridors, hands out in front of her, *entirely asleep*.'

'Did she wake her?' gasped Beanie.

'Of course not!' said Daisy. 'Everyone knows that you mustn't wake a sleepwalker. If you do, they'll get a frightful shock. They might even *die* from it. Poor Clementine, though. Sleepwalking is the most dreadful illness. You do things that you have no memory of afterwards. It's terribly dangerous for the sleepwalker – and for the people they live with.'

Beanie gasped, and Kitty squealed with excitement and dashed off ahead of us to where Sophie Croke-Finchley was walking with the twins, Rose and Jose Pritchett. I could tell she was off to spread the gossip about Clementine's condition – and that it would not be long before the whole house knew about it.

Sure enough, at dinner, the dining room was buzzing. 'What is all this nonsense?' snapped Clementine, banging down her plate onto the third-form table and looking very furious. 'I've just been asked by a shrimp whether it's true that I was the one who ate all the cake that went missing last week. I said of course I wasn't, and she said that I might not know, because I might have done it while I was asleep! What nonsense! What have you all been saying about me?'

'But isn't it true that you sleepwalk?' asked Beanie, confused.

'Of course I don't sleepwalk!' snarled Clementine. 'I've never sleepwalked in my life!'

Next to me, Daisy twitched with excitement. I could practically feel the jaws of her trap snapping shut. 'But if you don't sleepwalk,' she said innocently, 'then why did Betsy North tell me that she saw you in the corridor last night holding a tie?'

'What?' cried Clementine. 'But of course I wasn't—'

'Oh, so you *weren't* in the corridor outside our dorm last night?' asked Daisy.

'Well – no – I mean, yes, I was, but—'

'*You* took my tie?' growled Lavinia, standing up with her fists bunched. 'It was *you*?'

'No,' stammered Clementine. 'No, I – I was sleep-walking!'

'Odd,' said Daisy. 'I thought you'd *never sleepwalked in your life*?'

Clementine opened and closed her mouth like a landed fish. The whole of the table was staring at her. 'You *hit* me!' she shrieked at last. 'You *deserved* it!'

Lavinia gave a low animal roar and surged forward at her, fists flailing, and then the scene dissolved into a really rather nasty argument.

But Daisy nudged me under the table. 'Watson,' she whispered, leaning close to my ear, 'I do believe that the Detective Society has solved its finest case yet!'

DAISY'S GUIDE TO DETECTING

Hello, it's Daisy again! After each and every one of our murder cases, Hazel asks that I write a sort of explanation of all the potentially difficult words that are in her casebooks (they are not difficult to *me*, you understand). Since we started the Detective Society I have written a *Guide to Deepdean*, a *Guide to Fallingford*, and even a *Guide to the Orient Express*. They are all excellent, and I hope you have read and appreciated them properly.

For this collection, Hazel has suggested I write another guide – a particularly special one. In the next few pages I shall explain to you how you can become a detective *almost* as good as me.

Picture the scene: a body has been discovered; an item has been stolen; a suspicious letter has been found. It is up to you to solve the case. But where should you begin?

27

First, establish the facts

In every mystery, the detective must discover the answers to five questions: *who, what, where, when* and *how*. Once they are solved, the case simply falls into place!

Let me give you an example. On Tuesday last week, an entire cream bun went missing from my plate during tea. As soon as its loss was discovered, my brain began to work. I was the victim, but also the detective. What else did I know, and what did I need to find out?

Who? (Who did it?)

Unknown. This is what I wanted to discover! It must have been a member of our boarding house, as I didn't see anyone unknown enter the room during the meal.

What? (What happened?)

This was easier. The unknown culprit had stolen my bun, presumably because they wanted to eat it themselves.

Where? (Where was the scene of the crime?)

The House Dining Room, on the fourth formers' table. This narrowed down the suspect list considerably. The culprit could only have been someone with a reason to be at the table at the time of the theft – so either a fourth former, or the prefect on duty at the table.

When? (**When did the crime take place, and what else was happening?**)

Last Tuesday afternoon, just after a rather punishing Games lesson. It was a beastly crime because I was particularly hungry. I also recalled that, a minute before the bun went missing, the conversation had become very heated. The other fourth-form dorm had lost our hockey game, and Sophie Croke-Finchley had been loudly upset about it. We had all turned to look at her – and when I turned back, my bun was gone.

How? (**How could the thief have carried out the crime?**)

My answer to *when* helped me to work out *how*. Sophie had distracted me, and knowing the rivalry between our dorms, I suspected that she had done so on purpose. But who might she have been working with? The twins, Rose and Jose Pritchett, usually work together, so it was unlikely to be them. But there is one more member of the dorm who is friends with Sophie who dislikes me, and who might have tried to get one over on me (forgetting, of course, that no one tricks the Honourable Daisy Wells for long) . . .

As you will see, there was only one possible culprit: Clementine Delacroix, Sophie's dorm mate and our dorm's sworn enemy. I forced her to stand up and turn out her pockets – and the bun was revealed, wrapped in Clementine's handkerchief. Clementine gave it back to me at once, and that evening I had my revenge – I crept into the other dorm while Clementine and her associates were at toothbrushes and gave her an apple pie bed. This is an excellent prank, where you secretly fold an undersheet back on itself so the person can't get their legs into the bed properly, and I advise you all to learn it. You never know when it may come in useful.

Creating a suspect list

The mystery of the stolen cream bun was so easy that a suspect list was not needed. But most cases are more difficult, and then a suspect list is simply crucial.

Begin by thinking of everyone who may have had the opportunity to commit the crime. Even the most unlikely people can be suspects! Make your Secretary write them all down in order, and for each suspect note down the following information:

Motive: Can you think of a reason why this suspect may have wanted to commit the crime? If you are investigating a murder, it may be a question of revenge, or hatred. Perhaps there is a great sum of money involved, or jewels. Or could the victim have known a dangerous secret that the suspect was desperate to cover up?

Alibi: This is a Latin word that means *elsewhere* (now you can tell your friends that and feel particularly clever). An alibi is proof that a suspect could not have been committing the crime because they were somewhere else when it took place. For example, imagine there was a murder in a park at three o'clock on a Thursday afternoon. If one of your suspects was in a shop buying a new hat at that time, and the shopkeeper can corroborate their story (a detective word that means *agree*) with a receipt or similar physical proof, then they have an alibi and can be ruled out. But beware tricks and deception! Sometimes a criminal will make up a false alibi to put a detective off the scent.

Notes: These are any details you know about a suspect that may help either eliminate or convict them. Make sure anything you note is precise and thorough – if you write down something false or vague, it may confuse both you and your case!

Investigating the scene of the crime

This is always important, and particularly vital if you are investigating a theft or a murder.

Note that you'll need a stiff upper lip if it's a murder you're dealing with – bodies and blood *should* be no barrier to truth and justice, but in practice they are rather upsetting, especially to Hazel. However, you must simply swallow your fear and start hunting for clues.

Does anything seem out of place? Has anything been moved, documents rifled through or books searched? Could something be missing from the room, and if so, has it left any traces? Look for rings of dust where ornaments have sat or faded places on a wall where pictures were hanging.

And if nothing is missing, has anything been left behind by the culprit? This might be an item of clothing, a cigarette butt, or even – if you're very lucky – the murder weapon. Or perhaps something subtler – a strand of hair, a spot of blood, finger- or footprints. More on prints later, as they're utterly invaluable.

Tip: Keep a paper bag on your person at all times, for storing any clues that you might find. Make sure you wear gloves, or wrap your sleeve around your hand so that you don't leave prints on evidence!

Studying the body

If the body is still there, this is a vital opportunity to find out exactly *how* the victim was killed. Make sure that you do NOT touch the body, because the police will be very cross with you for destroying evidence. However, remember to look for wounds or other suspicious marks. What is the victim wearing? This may tell you where they have just been, or where they were planning to go. And you may observe other clues on the body too: an incriminating letter, or a locket that reveals a scandalous love affair, for example.

Measuring footprints and taking fingerprints

As I mentioned earlier, prints can be the clues that help you to solve the crime once and for all. Taking prints from a crime scene is a vital skill for any detective.

Measuring footprints

You will need:

- A long piece of string
- A pencil
- A magnifying glass

Of course, the presence of the suspect who left the footprint doesn't necessarily mean they are guilty, but it certainly places them under direct suspicion.

Observe the area using your **magnifying glass**. If you spot a footprint, hold the **piece of string** taut along it. Then, on the string, mark off the length of the footprint using your **pencil**.

Now, this is the tricky part. You'll also need to measure the shoes of your suspects, to see if any match the length of the footprint. It's imperative not to get caught – I'd suggest a distraction from your Vice-President and a quick dive under the table.

Taking fingerprints

You will need:

– Powder: for example, talcum powder or women's face powder. Flour works equally well.
– A small brush, such as a make-up brush
– Clear tape
– Dark paper

On surfaces where you suspect there may be finger-prints, use your small brush to lightly dust them with your powder. Try not to spill too much of it! You should see the faint impression of a print, which you can then match to the fingerprints of your suspect. Gently and carefully press the tape over the print, once the powder has made it appear. To take fingerprints from your suspects to look for a match, simply repeat the process on an area you are certain they have recently touched. A glass, a plate or a shiny table are perfect for this. Remember not to get caught!

Interviewing witnesses

Did anyone see the crime take place? If it happened in a busy street, for instance, it's vital to find out if anyone was about just before or after, and go and talk to them. This could lead to crucial clues (though do beware of witnesses who may be lying!).

Tip: Use the shrimps! *Shrimps* is our word for the youngest girls at Deepdean. As no one ever notices them, they can be a most useful source of information. Like Kitty, they see a great deal. The shrimps can be your eyes and ears around your school, and are often experts on any rumours flying around. Be firm but charming – this is a technique that also works with Hazel – and you'll find it easy to win them over.

But it's always important to remember that anything you tell the shrimps will be passed around the school, so make sure they don't know too much about what you're doing!

Eavesdropping

This is how you'll find your most valuable information. At Deepdean, eavesdropping during lessons or bun-break is the surest way of discovering evidence – and also the juiciest gossip.

To begin with, find a good hiding place. This should be a spot from where you can hear perfectly well what is happening, yet also remain completely unseen. Suitable places to eavesdrop include cupboards, behind doors and under desks or tables.

Now, I have a particularly good memory, and an uncanny ability to retain information. But if you're like Hazel, you may need to jot down what you hear in your casebook as it's being said. This will avoid any . . . disagreements, later on.

Tip: Don't be afraid to fake illness to allow yourself more time to eavesdrop. (Hazel and I once made ourselves truly, properly ill when we were investigating the murder of Miss Bell, using ipecac syrup. It was jolly effective, but Hazel says I mustn't encourage you to do this yourself.) If you go to Deepdean, you'll know that the San – the place we go to when we're ill to be looked after by our nurse, Mrs Minn – is also an absolutely perfect place for eavesdropping. You may overhear all sorts of useful information from your sick bed. Just make sure you escape again in time for bunbreak!

Tracking

This is a special detective term for following your suspects. Tracking is a dangerous and difficult art that requires practice. If you're lucky, you'll hear some useful conversations, or observe some suspicious behaviour. Always maintain a safe distance from your suspect, try to keep out of sight and *don't* look as though you're following them. If you need to, wear a disguise. If all else fails, know when to run!

Knowing your surroundings and blending in

When detecting, it is vital to observe the environment you are in, and to behave accordingly. If detectives draw attention to themselves, they could place themselves or the rest of their Society in grave danger. Blending in is absolutely key.

Because I am a detective through and through, I always take care to blend in, both at Deepdean and during holidays, even when I am not on a case. After all, you simply never know when a crime is likely to occur, and if you are on the spot, looking and behaving as though you ought to be there, you will be able to begin detecting immediately.

Here are some rules that I live by, which I have tried to teach to Hazel:

Never be late. Or, if you are, always be ready with the perfect excuse.

Never appear too intelligent. I doubt this will apply to many of you, but for me, it's terribly important to maintain an image of average cleverness. This helps me seem approachable and ordinary.

Never be caught while you are out of lessons. Notice I don't say that you should never *be* out of lessons. You must simply never get *caught*. This is the perfect time to engage in some sly detection.

Be as charming and engaging as you possibly can, especially with grown-ups. A winning smile and a ready laugh will go a long way to getting everyone on your side – crucial when investigating a case.

Practising the art of distraction

Lessons are the perfect opportunity to pass notes. But for goodness' sake, be subtle about it. This is something Beanie is particularly useless at. But because I know this fact, I was once able to use it very cleverly to help me solve a case. I passed an extremely funny note to Beanie, she laughed and caught the prefect's attention, and I quickly used the distraction to pass another, far more important note to Hazel. I really am quite brilliant.

~~Dealing with Hazel~~

Hazel made me take this bit out.

Re-creating the crime

Hazel and I have used the following technique for every murder case we have investigated so far, and it has never failed to further our investigation.

First you must know exactly where and in what position the body was found. If you've been vigilant in your activities since the murder, this should be easy.

Get one of the members of your Society to play the part of the victim, and the rest to be the suspects. Everything should then proceed – according to the information you have gathered – exactly as it happened on the day or night of the murder.

Use a wristwatch to time everything to the exact second, and ensure that every member of the Society knows what they're doing. If you're lucky, you should be able to find out the following:

Whether any suspects can be eliminated. It may be that timings make it impossible for a certain suspect to have committed the murder. This means that they can be struck off your suspect list.

Further details of how the victim was murdered. If the crime has been recreated correctly, you may be able to find out more information on exactly how the murder happened. The victim may have fallen in a particular way, or died at a particular moment within your time frame.

The murder weapon. If you haven't discovered the murder weapon already, recreating the crime may reveal to you what objects were to hand when the murder was committed. Even small, unlikely items could be *part* of a weapon. Never, ever ignore a clue.

Confronting your murderer — also known as the 'Denouement'

Unfortunately, one must usually involve the police at some point. When Hazel and I have put so much work into solving a case, it's galling when someone else takes the glory, but the annoying fact is that we are technically still children and cannot arrest murderers ourselves.

However, although you must have the police present when you confront your murderer, you should try to make sure that they don't interfere until the very end, when it is their job to wrestle the culprit to the ground and take them away in handcuffs. The whole thing must be as dramatic and theatrical as possible.

When holding a denouement, try to:

Ensure that all your suspects are gathered together. For country house murders, drawing rooms are ideal. For murders on trains, you should use the dining carriage, and so on.

Speak clearly and slowly. Take time to pause and stare meaningfully at people. This will alarm them, and may force a confession.

Draw proceedings out for as long as possible. Savour the moment, discuss the case and make sure to address each suspect in turn. It is important that everyone realizes how brilliant you are.

Make them confess. As soon as you accuse the criminal, they should confess – or at least, they ought to. If they do not, they are not being very sporting.

This concludes my Guide. I hope you have found it useful and inspiring. Good luck, detectives, and remember – although you can never be as brilliant as me (and sometimes Hazel), you can learn to be almost as good.

THE CASE OF THE BLUE VIOLET

Being an account of

The Case of Violet Darby,
an investigation by the Wells and Wong Detective Society
(mainly Daisy Wells).

Written by Daisy Wells
(Detective Society President), aged 14.

Begun Thursday 26th September 1935
and finished the next day.

Here is a case that Daisy and I solved just before the beginning of our Bonfire Night Murder. Daisy is terribly proud of it — it is the first case she has ever written out herself. I thought she might want to write up one of our murder mysteries after she was done with it, but she said it would take far too long and she would get terribly bored and simply skip to the denouement. I'm quite glad about that. The murder mysteries, by now, feel like mine.

—Hazel Wong

I

This is the account of a case that I solved almost entirely on my own. It seemed very puzzling at first (at least, some people were puzzled), but I solved it as quick as anything. That is because I am the Honourable Daisy Wells, President of the Detective Society. I am fourteen at the moment, in the fourth form at Deepdean School for Girls. This is a bother, as it means I have to pretend to be an ordinary schoolgirl. But soon I shall be twenty, and then I shall become the world's greatest consulting detective – like Sherlock Holmes, only real. I shall set up my own detective agency with Hazel Wong. She is my Vice-President, and I suppose my best friend too, although that sounds less official. I haven't asked her yet, but I'm quite sure she'll agree. Hazel is a very good sort of person, a true brick. Sometimes she does think for herself rather, just as though she ran the Detective Society instead of me, but I have tried to train her out of it. Largely she does listen.

Hazel usually writes down our cases (we have had three real murders so far, as well as quite a few littler cases, which is far more than most grown-ups), but I have been telling her that if I wanted to, I could note one down as well. Hazel didn't believe me at the time. She made Hazel's Disbelieving Face – which is pursed lips and very straight eyebrows – and I'm sure she thought that was the end of it. Now, though, I mean to prove her wrong. I shall write up the Case of the Blue Violet (that is my name for it, and I think it very good and quite amusing), and I will do it just as well as she could, and twice as quickly. Hazel always spends far too long describing people talking to each other, and when I read her notes I have to skim.

Hazel is leaning over my shoulder and looking dis-approving again as she reads what I have written. I don't know why – I am only being truthful. As I was saying, this is the story of one of our cases. It is not a murder (which is a pity), but it is rather interesting. It is about what happened when one of the prettiest Big Girls, Violet Darby, came up to me at bunbreak a week after the beginning of term and said, 'Please help me, Daisy Wells. I'm in the most dreadful trouble, and you are my only hope!'

Hazel (still leaning) says that I am inventing that. Well, perhaps Violet didn't say those words exactly – but she *was* upset, and she *did* ask for my help. Now, it is true that the Detective Society is secret. At least, it's *supposed* to be, although I am concerned that *some* members may *not be as good as I am* at keeping it so. But Violet knew about it, and about me, for one very good reason: her cousin is King Henry. King Henry, whose real name is Henrietta Trilling, was our Head Girl last year, and we helped her during our first real case, the Murder of Miss Bell. (You may read about *that* in one of Hazel's casebooks; the one with the blue cover.) Quite obviously, King Henry had reason to recommend our services, and so when the problem of the letter arose, Violet knew that I was absolutely the best person at Deepdean to ask. And Hazel too, of course.

After she had approached us and asked for our help, Violet was quite upset. She stood there squashing her bun in her hands instead of eating it. We – Hazel mostly – got Violet to calm down and sat her on the wall. Then, once she had stopped hiccupping and wiping her cheeks, I told her to explain herself.

This is the story she gave us. I am not embroidering this part, because the facts of the case are vitally important for a detective to understand. And I must explain properly, so that you can see how I got to my conclusion.

Violet Darby lives in Gloucestershire, on a country estate quite like Fallingford (my family's house). In July of this year, her father sent her over to the Graves Estate, next door but one, to meet its new owner, Lord Graves. Now, 'Lord Graves' is not really a name. Just like Daddy, who is called Lord Hastings as well as George Wells, it is just a title. It is passed on from person to person, like a ring or a coat. The old Lord Graves had been *very* old, so old that he died in the spring and gave his title to his nephew, Mr Eastham.

Before he became Lord Graves, Mr Eastham had lived in America for several years. He had a wife there, and also one son, Edward Eastham. Edward was nineteen, and had lived in America with his father and gone to school there ever since he was Hazel's and my age. But now his father was back in England, and in possession of a really quite enormous estate, and Edward was home in England with him for good. He was now all grown up, and did not even have an American accent to make him the least bit unmarriageable. And so Violet's father naturally thought that Violet ought to meet Edward.

Violet had not really liked this idea – she is not the sort of person who listens to her father – but all the same she rode up to the house one sunny day in July. She was rather dreading it, and the thought of Edward, and so when she was shown into the morning room she felt leaden inside – but only Lord Graves was there. He looked rather bothered to see her (Violet's father had not telephoned ahead to say she was coming). He told her that Edward had gone out, but that he'd be home shortly – if she liked, she could wait for him outside. Lord Graves was busy with some letters, and trying to get rid of her, and Violet saw that. She went hurrying to the front door, and freedom, hoping like anything that she would miss Edward and be able to go home without any bother – but as she was standing on the front steps, up drove a car and out jumped Edward Eastham.

He was not at all what Violet had been imagining. She had been expecting a rather chinless idiot, but the boy walking towards her was nice-looking, tall and athletic, and he stopped her still. Her heart beat fast (even when she described him to us, her cheeks went pink) and she realized that she was very glad she had met him after all. She waved at Edward, and he waved back – and five minutes later, Violet Darby was bowling through the countryside in Edward Eastham's car, in love.

After that, Edward and Violet went driving together most days. She would leave her house on foot, meet him in a lane, and off they would go. When her father asked, she gave him the vague impression that she hadn't cared for Edward (she did not explain this, but I understood why – it is such a bore, pleasing one's parents). The times she couldn't get out, she sent her maid over to the Graves Estate with letters and tokens (locks of hair and soppy poems and all the silly things that people in love share), and she would get letters back.

It was all going terribly well until Violet had to go back to Deepdean.

She said goodbye to Edward, and she was driven back to school by her father's chauffeur. Of course, the very first thing she did when she arrived was to write to Edward – and two days later, she received a reply. And it threw her into the most enormous confusion.

I am making Hazel copy down what Edward's letter said here, because it is both important and rather shocking.

September 23rd 1935

Dear Miss Darby,

I am puzzled. I am afraid that I have never met you, and I certainly do not know any of the instances to which you refer in your letter. Have you contacted me in error?

Yours sincerely,

Edward Eastham

She wrote back at once, by return of post, asking him what he meant by it. I think she rather hoped it was some sort of joke, for Edward had been quite fond of joking, even though he was in love.

The next day, though, the following letter was in her pigeon hole at House.

September 25th 1935

Miss Darby,

There seems to be something wrong with you. I have never met you and I certainly do not know what brings you to write to me so familiarly. Please stop all communications at once.

Yours,

E. Eastham

At this point Violet broke down in tears again, which I thought was rather foolish of her. However, I made sure to have Hazel comfort her. It is not good to put clients off, and I was most intrigued. I decided to get the obvious questions out of the way first.

'Are you sure it was the right address?' I asked, when Violet had stopped weeping for a moment.

'Y-yes!' said Violet, gulping. 'I made sure it was. And he says his name, there – it *is* Edward, it has to be! I know his handwriting, as well. Why is he lying? Doesn't he like me any more? Is . . . What if there is someone else?'

'That can't be it,' said Hazel, and frowned. 'If there was another girl, he simply wouldn't write back.'

Hazel can be quite wise sometimes.

'My Vice-President is quite right,' I said. 'It doesn't fit. No, there must be another explanation. Is he ill? Perhaps his mind has gone.'

'He wasn't ill when I left!' said Violet. 'He couldn't be – so quickly! Oh, but what if he is? Edward!' She began to cry again.

'Does he have a twin?' I asked. I was thinking about the cases I have read in my crime novels. Twins are often a very useful explanation – although they are rather a cheat. I don't think much of authors who use them.

Violet shook her head. 'He's an only child!' she said. 'Everyone knows it.'

I wondered about a *secret* twin – and then I saw Hazel's face, and thought perhaps I was jumping to conclusions. 'But he's written you letters before?' I asked. 'May we see them?'

It was, of course, the perfect question. Violet looked hesitant – I knew why, of course: because of all the soppy things that were in them – but at last I told her that if she didn't show us, we couldn't solve her case. She pulled a packet of letters out of her pinafore skirt, going pink. (For some reason, when I looked at Hazel, she had gone rather red herself.)

Violet skimmed through them, hardly having to look (they were very creased and thumbed; she had clearly read them very often), and at last chose one to open. Hazel and I peered at it. It was in the same simple schoolboy copperplate as the others we had seen:

Graves Estate, 14th August 1935

My lovely Violet,

    I miss you every moment we are apart. I know I do tease, but I really can't imagine a world without you. We mustn't let anything break us apart. After all,

> *Love is not love*
> *Which alters when it alteration finds,*
> *Or bends with the remover to remove:*
> *O no; it is an ever-fixed mark,*
> *That looks on tempests, and is never*
> *   shaken;*
> *It is the star to every wandering bark,*
> *Whose worth's unknown, although his*
> *   height be taken.*

Your love,
E

It was very soppy, just as I had been expecting. But there was something in it – only a very little thing, but enough for a keen detective mind like mine to be alerted. I felt my brain race. Could it be? If so – why, the case might be over almost before it had begun.

'Violet,' I said. 'I have had a thought. Can I come with you, while you use the telephone?'

'But I don't need to use the telephone,' said Violet, proving that she was not as clever as me – which, really, is not surprising.

'*Yes you do*,' I said. 'Or at least, *you say you do*.'

'She's got a lead in the case. She wants to phone someone to confirm it,' whispered Hazel to Violet.

'Oh! Why didn't you say so before? Meet me at lunch time and I'll get you into Matron's office,' said Violet.

Hazel made a face at me, which I ignored. She is sometimes far too soft with clients for her own good.

II

At lunch time Violet took me into Matron's study to use the telephone.

'What shall I say if she asks what we're doing here?' she kept on asking, terribly worried. It was an awful bother to keep her focused and explain that, as she was a Big Girl, Matron would not even ask.

I was exhausted by the time I picked up the receiver and heard the operator's voice.

'Hello,' I said. 'Fallingford two-four-three, please.' It is always good to be polite. It makes people wonderfully willing to give you things.

'Of course,' said the operator.

There was a click, and a few whirrs, and then our butler Chapman's voice echoed down the wire to me, saying, 'Hello?'

'Chapman!' I said. 'It's Daisy. Can you get Hetty for me, please?'

Hetty, my maid, is another true brick. If she were not a grown-up she would be an excellent member of the Detective Society – a far more worthy one than *some* people. But despite her age, she can still be useful, especially if one wants to find out some information quickly. I told Hetty what I wanted her to find out and tell me (I will not say it here, because I am building suspense, and also giving you a chance to solve the case: perhaps you may not be as brilliant a detective as I am, but you may as well try), and she said she would get it to me as soon as she could.

'Borrow the money from Chapman,' I said, to punish him for listening. (I knew he was standing next to Hetty; I could hear him breathing.)

'Miss D—' Chapman began, offended – but I put the receiver down as quick as anything, so I would not have to hear him scolding me.

'Why did you want to know that?' asked Violet, looking troubled. I turned to Hazel, and saw that she understood. Her brow was wrinkled up.

'A good detective never reveals her methods,' I said. 'Not before we give you the answer, anyway. Hazel, don't tell.'

Hazel pressed her lips together. I did think that the look she gave me was unfair. I am still her President, after all. This year she sometimes forgets that.

'Do you know?' she asked me later.

'Of course,' I said. 'Even before Hetty confirms it. Do you?'

'Of course. How will you tell her?'

'I shall think of something,' I said. 'Tomorrow.'

To be quite honest, I hadn't thought – but when Hazel asked, tomorrow was still an awfully long way away. I went over the case in my head, lining the details up like pebbles on a wall. It was all very satisfying. I think some people feel this way when they look at a painting or hear music, which makes me think that some people are awfully strange.

The next morning, at breakfast, there was a telegram waiting for me. It was very brief.

THREE STOP GARDENER VALET CHAUFFEUR
STOP BE GOOD STOP HETTY STOP

Hazel and I looked at each other. We both knew that the case was solved.

'What are you up to?' asked our dorm mate Lavinia, chewing on a piece of toast. 'You look odd.'

'They look *mysterious*,' said our other dorm mate Kitty, grinning. I glared at her. Kitty is dreadful at keeping secrets. It's really quite offensive.

'Yes, it's *fascinating*,' I said. 'My maid, telling me about *staff*.'

That shut Kitty up, as I knew it would. She curled her lip and turned away to talk to our friend Beanie. Of course, it never occurred to her to ask why my maid should be sending me an urgent telegram about staff. People never really do see what's in front of them. It's terribly lucky – it means that I can do almost anything I like.

III

In the bunbreak queue that morning, I nodded at Violet. She went pale, but she nodded back, and as soon as we were all out on the lawn she came to find us, doing a very good impression of a Big Girl condescending to speak to two fourth formers.

'We know the answer,' I said.

'Oh,' said Violet. 'Tell me!'

'We shall,' I said. 'We want paying, though.'

'Of course,' said Violet. 'Anything! Only – tell me what's wrong with Edward!'

'Nothing's wrong with him,' I said. 'Only – the person you know as Edward isn't Edward *Eastham* at all. He's the Easthams' chauffeur. That's who you're in love with. You've never met Edward Eastham, and he's never met you. Isn't it obvious? And that'll cost you those nice cakes that you've got stored in your tuck box, all four of them – oh, and two favours, one for each of us, whenever we need them.'

Violet dropped her biscuit. 'Oh!' she said. 'I say! It can't – it can't be true!'

'Of course it is,' I said. I felt frustrated. Why don't people understand, when I speak to them clearly? 'Hazel, explain!'

'It does make sense,' said Hazel gently. 'Edward wasn't in the house with Lord Graves when you arrived, was he? The first time you ever saw the boy you think of as Edward was when he got out of the car – and you never saw him with any of the Graves family, because you were meeting in secret. And you never told us he introduced himself as Edward Eastham. How did you *know* that's who he was?'

'But he said— He— Oh!' said Violet. 'I asked him if he was Edward, and he said yes, but – oh, never his last name!'

'Exactly!' I said. 'You only assumed. You thought that he was driving *his* car – but again, how could you *know*? How could you be sure that what you were seeing wasn't something else – a chauffeur who had just come back from taking his master to an event?'

'But . . . he didn't *say* he was!'

'Of course he didn't! Why would he? He didn't want to contradict a lady – and then it was too late.'

'*Too late?*' repeated Violet. Her eyes had gone very wide.

'He had already fallen in love with you, of course,' I said. 'Of course he loved you – look at his letter! Oh, Hazel, explain again.'

'He copied down poetry for you,' said Hazel. 'All those nice words! He was afraid that when you found out you'd be cross, and leave him – that's what he meant by *We mustn't let anything break us apart*. And it wasn't just what he said, but what he did – he spent all summer with you. He must love you very much.'

'Of course, when it was your maid going to the Graves Estate, he could stop her and take the letters before they ever reached the real Edward,' I went on. 'Then, when he wrote back, he disguised his handwriting to look like Edward's – just in case. He would have seen plenty of samples in notes and so on, and really it wouldn't be hard. That copperplate of his – every schoolboy in the world learns how to write like that.

And these days, even chauffeurs are very educated. The only difference between the way the boy you're in love with and the real Edward write their letters is very small – but, of course, I noticed it at once.'

Violet's mouth was hanging open.

'*The date!*' I said impatiently. 'Didn't you see? Now, the real Edward Eastham went to America when he was already quite old, so we know he doesn't have an accent. But he went to *school* there, and so he would have picked up certain American habits – like writing the date all wrong, with the month first. In the most recent letters you got, the date was like that. But in the romantic one you showed us, that your boyfriend had written to you during the summer, the *day* was first, and then the month. Two different ways of setting out a letter; two different people, with two different backgrounds.'

'But if— But how—' Violet began, and I saw that she was still struggling with the problem.

'The *real* Edward Eastham only began to write to you when you went back to Deepdean—' Hazel began.

'Because your letters went through the *normal* post!' I finished for her impatiently. 'Your boyfriend had no chance to intercept them – the postman would give them straight to the valet every morning. That's how we knew that your boyfriend wasn't the valet, by the way. There are three young men on the estate apart from

Edward Eastham: the gardener, the valet and the chauffeur. The gardener was all wrong, because the boy you described wasn't dirty or scruffy. It could have been the valet or the chauffeur – but your letters from school went to the *real* Edward, and if it had been the valet, he would have taken them, not given them to Edward. And, of course, the valet wouldn't have been very likely to be driving about in a car. No, it all fits. You've fallen in love with Lord Graves's chauffeur, not his son. What do you think about that?'

Violet had gone pale. 'But . . .' she whispered. 'What am I going to do?'

'You ought to be pleased!' I said. 'After all, your father will be furious. And as to what you do with your boyfriend – tell him you know, of course. And if he doesn't mind, you can marry him.'

'Marry him!'

'If you go to Scotland, you can do it without your parents knowing anything about it,' I said. 'Haven't you read books? I don't see why you shouldn't marry him. He knows poetry, and he can drive. He's probably far better than Edward Eastham.'

'Daisy!' said Hazel. 'She doesn't even know what he's called!'

'Names aren't important,' I said. 'After all, *you've* got two, and you were my best friend for years before I found out your Chinese one.'

Violet was crying and laughing at the same time, so I thought it best to leave her to herself for a while. I winked at Hazel and nodded my head, and we slipped away together.

'Another case solved,' I said. 'Rather good work on my part.' Hazel sighed. 'The Detective Society's part, then! But it really was mostly me.'

'All right,' said Hazel, rolling her eyes. 'This time it was.'

I slipped my arm through hers. Hazel is good to lean against – she may be short, but she is comfortingly solid. 'Aren't people soppy when they get old?' I said. 'All this love nonsense. I'm sure I don't understand it. Don't fall in love, will you?'

'Of course I won't,' said Hazel.

IV

I was glad we had agreed that. And, all in all, I was pleased with the case. It may have been the Detective Society's quickest ever. It was all neatly wrapped up – and even more so the next Monday, when we came up to our dorm after lunch to discover a box of Violet's delicious-looking cakes on my bed. Next to them was a note.

It read:

His name is Ed Higgins. He said yes. Don't tell Daddy.
  Violet

Hazel and I grinned at each other. We are really becoming rather good detectives.

THE GOLDEN AGE OF DETECTIVE STORIES WITH ROBIN STEVENS

For this section I've decided to take over from my Detective Society to tell you a bit more about where and when the sort of mystery stories I write come from. This is something I know a lot about – I actually wrote a very long essay about it at university. Even then I knew I wanted to write real detective stories myself. I'd already written the first draft of *Murder Most Unladylike*, but I wasn't brave enough to show it to anyone yet!

I won't write out that essay again, but I will try to explain to you about where detective novels came from, and why they became so incredibly popular during the 1930s, the time when Daisy and Hazel began their careers as detectives. Detective novels from the thirties are also known as 'Golden Age' detective novels – named because of how many people were writing mysteries then, and how good they were!

Obviously, murder has been around since . . . well, since for ever. It's not new at all! But the *detective*, the person whose job it is to catch criminals (especially murderers), was only properly invented in the Victorian era. The French got there first, when a man called Vidocq set up his own detective agency in the 1830s. He was enormously brilliant (he was the first person EVER to analyse footprints!), and he became a bit of a hero all over the world.

In fact, he was so famous that Edgar Allan Poe (an author known for horror stories like *The Telltale Heart* and *The Fall of the House of Usher*, which you should not read alone or at night) decided to create a character based on him. That character was C. Auguste Dupin, and the story he first appears in is *The Murders in the Rue Morgue*. Dupin, like Vidocq, solves crimes using intellect, deduction and logic. He almost seems able to read the mind of his companion, a man who narrates the story as well as helping Dupin solve the crime. (The crime's solution, by the way, is totally ridiculous and unguessable. Poe invented the fictional detective, but not quite the modern mystery story . . .)

The first full-length detective novel in English was technically *The Moonstone* by Wilkie Collins. But while it's a fantastic, exciting book, and there is definitely a detective in it (Sergeant Cuff, who just wants to retire and grow roses), there's something about it that still doesn't fit our idea of what a mystery should be. It's *very* long, it's narrated by about five different people and there isn't actually a murder.

The world was waiting for a really great fictional detective. And (I'm sure you can guess what I'm about to say) it got one in 1888, when Arthur Conan Doyle's story *A Study in Scarlet* introduced us to the consulting detective Sherlock Holmes.

Holmes has quite a lot of Dupin about him – the logical brain, the mind-reading tricks, the friendly companion – but he's also unique. He's been fascinating crime fans (including the Honourable Daisy Wells) for over one hundred years, because he's just *so good* at what he does. When you read a Holmes story, you feel as though you're *nearly* following along, that the solution is *just* out of your reach – and then Sherlock reveals the truth with a flourish like a magician.

Which pretty much brings us to the 1930s. Now, the thirties was a strange, strange decade to live in. All the grown-ups had already lived through the First World War. It became pretty clear pretty quickly that more bad things were on their way. But (especially if you lived in Britain) you *did not want to talk about those bad things*. What people wanted instead were ways to escape. They wanted to read books that would help them feel as though the world was safe, understandable and fixable, even though it was full of danger.

So obviously they read murder mysteries.

That sounds ridiculous, but just think about it. Murder mysteries are pretty much the safest stories ever. There is only ever *one* crime (or set of crimes), committed by *one* person (or group of people). That criminal is bad, and everyone else is good, and the detective *always* works out who the bad person is and removes them from the scene, so the rest of the characters can go on living their lives without worry. See?

People in the 1930s read so many murder mysteries that the mystery business *boomed*. Most of the really successful authors were British women, although there were famous writers from other countries too – the Belgian writer Georges Simenon, for instance. These authors – you'll read more about them in the next section – took the big personality of Sherlock Holmes, added to it the drama of *The Moonstone*, and then added one more really important thing: RULES. They made the murder-mystery plot a formula, and that made it feel really nice and comforting as well as exciting.

In every murder mystery there has to be a murder. A detective has to solve it. There have to be suspects, who have to be ruled out one by one (with a few red herrings, also known as fake clues, dropped in to mislead the reader and detective for a while), and at the end the detective has to unmask the murderer and take them away to the nice safe prison. If you read lots of novels from the Golden Age, you'll notice that they start to seem similar – plots, characters and crimes all turn up again and again. English country houses, lords and ladies, murders at dinner parties, locked rooms, handsome scoundrels, fabulous jewels, poisoned chocolates, mysterious knives, untraceable poisons . . . every Golden Age detective novel feels familiar as well as new, because they were written that way on purpose.

There were so many Golden Age detective novelists that most of them were friends as well as rivals, and some of them even formed a club together. The Detective Society and its pledge is (slightly) inspired by the real-life Detection Club founded by Agatha Christie, Dorothy Sayers and their friends. The Club's members would spend evenings together, discussing real and made-up crimes and testing each other's detective skills. They also spent a lot of time making up sets of rules about what a crime writer should and shouldn't put in their books. The rules I knew about when I was Daisy and Hazel's age were by a man called Ronald Knox, and they were what I was thinking about when I wrote *Murder Most Unladylike*. Some of Knox's rules are serious, and some are silly. Even now, whenever I start a new book I think about these rules and decide which I want to follow, and which I want to break. They're listed here, along with my comments . . .

Ronald Knox's Rules

1. The criminal must be someone mentioned in the early part of the story, but must not be anyone whose thoughts the reader has been allowed to follow.

This is one I always follow. I don't like the idea of introducing a murderer towards the end – I want my killer to be someone the reader, as well as my detectives, knows very well and possibly even likes!

2. All supernatural or preternatural agencies are ruled out as a matter of course.

I follow this as well. My books don't have ghosts, though I love dropping in characters who believe in (or seem to believe in) them. Hazel is very scared of ghosts, and that's partly because I was thinking about this rule.

3. Not more than one secret room or passage is allowable.

I don't think I've ever broken this rule . . . though my readers, as well as Daisy and Hazel, know about one very important secret passage in my books . . .

4. No hitherto undiscovered poisons may be used, nor any appliance which will need a long scientific explanation at the end.

I follow this one too! All my poisons are real and (at the time Daisy and Hazel are investigating) easy to get hold of, and all my murder methods are quite easy to follow. It's just the killers who are hard to work out!

5. No Chinese person must figure in the story.

This is it. This is the rule that caused me sleepless nights as a child, and still upsets me today. I went to school with plenty of Chinese girls, and I could not understand why they weren't allowed to be in books. Ronald Knox was trying to make a joke here, but it's a very unfunny one. There aren't many Chinese people, or Indian people, or black people or . . . really anyone at all who isn't white in books, even in the present day, and this is both unrealistic and unfair. I wrote a detective novel with a Chinese heroine just to upset Ronald Knox, and now I am telling *you*, if you are reading this and you love writing, that you *must* write stories about Hazels as well as Daisys. That should be the new rule!

6. No accident must ever help the detective, nor must he ever have an unaccountable intuition which proves to be right.

I'm not sure about this one! I like making Hazel and Daisy stumble upon something that proves to be vital.

73

Of course, they also have to do great detective work, but a little serendipity can help too.

7. The detective must not himself commit the crime.

I often get asked whether I will make Hazel or Daisy the murderer in a future book, and this is my answer: I can't, because I want you to always love and trust them! It would be a different sort of story to the one I want to write.

8. The detective must not light on any clues which are not instantly produced for the inspection of the reader.

This one works for me as well. I always show you all the clues – I just try to make sure that you don't realize how important they are. I make you look the wrong way, like I'm doing a magic trick. Most of the time you never notice . . .

9. The stupid friend of the detective, the Watson, must not conceal any thoughts which pass through his mind; his intelligence must be slightly, but very slightly, below that of the average reader.

Another rule I don't agree with! Poor Watson wasn't stupid, and I think a stupid sidekick is a bit boring.

I wanted Hazel and Daisy to be just as clever as each other, in different ways – they complement each other, and they can't solve crimes without each other. I think my readers are just as smart as my detectives too!

10. Twin brothers, and doubles generally, must not appear unless we have been duly prepared for them.

There is one set of twins (sisters, not brothers, Ronald!) in my books, but my readers know all about them, so I've followed this rule so far. But will I always stick to it in future? Who knows . . . ?

So that's the Golden Age! I'm fascinated by it, and I wish I could go back in time to meet Agatha Christie and Dorothy Sayers and their friends. Of course, I'm not *exactly* writing the sort of books they were, because that would be boring (and it's already been done!), but they're big influences on me and my own mystery novels. In fact, it would be true to say that Daisy and Hazel wouldn't exist at all without them!

THE QUEENS OF CRIME

Daisy has decided that I (Hazel) should write this chapter. She says that it is only fair, although I think it's really because it involves research, and research makes Daisy bored. But I am glad, because even though these authors began as Daisy's favourites, they have become mine as well, and I liked finding out more about their lives.

Although all the murder cases I have written about so far are real, not made up, one day I think I should like to write a fictional mystery story myself, where no one real dies, and Daisy and I do not have to be afraid that the person who killed them would catch us before we catch them.

It is nice to know that all these authors are women, just like me. Although there are lots of men who write murder mysteries, these four are simply the best at it. This is why they are called the Queens of Crime.

Agatha Christie

Daisy says that Agatha Christie is the best author in the world, and I think I agree. She has invented the detectives Hercule Poirot and Miss Marple, written some of the most famous detective novels there are, and every new book she publishes seems more puzzling than the last.

She wasn't called Agatha Christie when she was born in 1890, of course – then she was Agatha Mary Clarissa Miller, and she lived in Devon. She loved writing even when she was very young (she started with poetry, but moved on to stories later). She also moved about a lot – first to France; then, in 1910, because of her mother's ill health, to Cairo, in Egypt. I am rather jealous. I would love to visit Egypt one day.

Agatha was very interested in the archaeological digs happening all around her. She loved mysteries and puzzles, and realized that a dig was just another sort of mystery. In archaeology, pieces of bone or pottery fit together to unlock the past – archaeologists are just like detectives, putting together clues to solve a mystery.

During the Great War Agatha worked as a nurse in Torquay, Devon, where she qualified as a dispenser. This is someone who mixes medicines and gives them out to patients. Dispensers have to know all about poisons (this makes Daisy very jealous; she wants to work in a dispensary just like Agatha, but I'm not sure whether that would really be a good idea). After the war ended she married Archie Christie, who had fought with the Royal Flying Corps (an older name for the Royal Air Force).

Then, in 1919, Agatha Christie (that was her name now!) fell ill. Her sister got cross with her for lying about in bed, and challenged her to write a detective story instead of just reading them. So Agatha wrote a book about a Belgian policeman called Hercule Poirot, who is invited to a house called Styles Court to *convalesce* (this means get better) after an illness. Then his host is poisoned, and Poirot has to solve the case.

Agatha Christie doesn't like Hercule Poirot, which seems very odd to me. I can't imagine disliking someone you made up yourself. I also feel rather sorry for Poirot. I know what it is like to be a stranger in Britain, and how it feels when English people laugh at you. Besides, Poirot is a very kind man – he is always looking after people. He's not cold, like Sherlock Holmes. He is sweet. I think if I was any detective in the world, I would be Poirot. Daisy, of course, would be Holmes.

The Mysterious Affair at Styles was Agatha Christie's first book, and today she is simply the most famous and best-selling author in the world. Her best-known mystery story so far (and Daisy's favourite) is *Murder on the Orient Express* – in fact, when we had to solve our own Orient

Express murder, Daisy used *Murder on the Orient Express* to help us do it. Of course, the two crimes were quite different, but all the same, the book came in useful!

Agatha Christie's life is sometimes almost as exciting as her books. In 1926 she was the centre of a real-life mystery. You'll find out more about that later (it is very exciting), but it ended with her divorcing her first husband, Archie, and becoming the wife of Max Mallowan, who is a real archaeologist. Today Agatha spends lots of time with him at his digs, so she works on archaeological mysteries as well as fictional ones.

Dorothy L. Sayers

Dorothy L. Sayers is very, very clever. I think she might be cleverer than Daisy, but Daisy says that is untrue. Her detective is Lord Peter Wimsey, and two of her most famous books are *Strong Poison* and *Gaudy Night*.

She was born in 1893 in the tiny village of Bluntisham-cum-Earith. (This sounds invented, like lots of English places, but it is real.) Her father was the vicar, and he taught her Latin when she was only six years old (do you see what I mean about her being clever?). She went to boarding school (though not to Deepdean, which is where Daisy and I go), and then she won a scholarship to Oxford University. She got a first-class honours degree in 1915 (the best you can get), but she was not allowed to actually have a degree, because she was a woman. This is not true of Oxford any more, but it is still the case at Cambridge, where Daisy's brother Bertie goes, and I think it is awful. Dorothy thinks so too, and that's why she set her book *Gaudy Night* in a women's college. It's a mystery (Daisy doesn't think it's a very good one), but it's also all about how unfair it is to be a woman, and clever, in a world that doesn't care for clever women.

While Dorothy was in Oxford she got a job as a secretary to Mr Blackwell, the owner of Blackwell's Bookshop. (One day our friend Robin Stevens will get a job in the same bookshop, but that's far in the future, long after Dorothy left.) Then Dorothy went to work for an advertising agency. She wrote slogans for – of all things – mustard and Guinness, and she disliked the agency so much that she used it as the setting for her book *Murder Must Advertise*.

Dorothy Sayers' most famous detective, Lord Peter Wimsey, rather reminds me of Daisy's Uncle Felix – or Uncle Felix if he was louder and more foolish – and her other detective, Harriet Vane, reminds me almost as much of Uncle Felix's wife. It's funny how much life is like books sometimes.

Ngaio Marsh

When I began to read about Ngaio Marsh (you say it like Nigh-o, by the way), I got rather excited. You see, although her books all seem very British, she is actually not British at all, just like me. She was born in New Zealand, and studied painting there, before she moved to Britain in 1928.

Her detective is Roderick Alleyn, who works for the Metropolitan Police. He's not an amateur like Poirot or Wimsey. Detecting is his job (I imagine him a bit like Inspector Priestley). He gets to use all the official tools of the police: proper fingerprint kits and photographs and official records, and so his mysteries take place in Scotland Yard as well as in big country houses. Ngaio Marsh also loves the theatre very much, and has set quite a few of her novels there.

That has made me realize that Daisy and I haven't yet come across a murder at the theatre. I wonder if we ever shall?

Margery Allingham

Margery Allingham began writing her detective stories when she was only just a bit older than Daisy and me – the age that Bertie and King Henry are now! Her most famous detective is Albert Campion, and two of her most famous novels are *Mystery Mile* and *Sweet Danger*.

She was born in London, but her family moved to Essex, and she later went to school in Cambridge. She was first paid for writing a story at the age of eight, and she wrote her first novel when she was nineteen.

Daisy loves Margery Allingham, but I am less sure, because most of her books are about ghosts as well as murders. She took part in seances when she was young, and borrowed the messages she was given by seventeenth-century pirates and smugglers to put in her books.

I hope ghosts do not really exist. I have never seen them, and I'm glad about that. I took part in a séance during the Case of the Murder of Miss Bell, and it turned out to be only a rather clever ruse of Daisy's. I also took part in one during our Orient Express case – and that also ended in a rather unexpected way! But Margery Allingham does believe in ghosts, and puts them in her books, and that unnerves me.

Margery's detective, Albert Campion, is upper class and British, but he has a servant called Lugg who's an ex-burglar, so he can be part of the criminal underworld as well. It's a clever thing to do – the best detectives should be able to move around in many different places.

DAISY'S TOP DETECTIVES

All right. Hazel did the boring bit about the lives of famous authors. I get the best bit – about the books themselves, and the people in them. I have made a list of my very favourite fictional detectives, and here it is for you to see. I would like to put myself at the top of the list but I can't because I am quite real.

10. Inspector Alan Grant

Alan Grant has only appeared in one book so far, *The Man in the Queue* by his author Josephine Tey, but I like him already and think he is quite a good detective. He is a police officer (which is boring – the police are boring; consulting detectives are far better), but despite that he solves his case very well.

9. Father Brown

Father Brown is a Catholic priest as well as being a detective. Again, this is dull and means that he is terribly moral all the time, but the stories that he is in (by G. K. Chesterton, if you want to look them up) are very clever indeed. Father Brown's best friend is a master criminal called Flambeau (Father Brown tries to save his soul, and it almost works), and I like him much better than Father Brown. If I was writing the Father Brown mysteries, I'd make them all about Flambeau.

8. Lord Peter Wimsey

Hazel is telling me that I have put him much too low down the list. It is true, as Hazel points out, that Wimsey is a bit like Uncle Felix, but in my opinion Uncle Felix is much better than Wimsey. I bet you anything that Dorothy Sayers knows Uncle Felix and has based Wimsey on him. Anyway, Wimsey is quite clever and I suppose an excellent detective, but he is too fond of quoting from boring old books, and sometimes the novels he appears in go on for *far* too long.

7. Roderick Alleyn

He is Ngaio Marsh's detective. He is a policeman again, but quite an inventive one, and he can be quite witty at times. Almost as witty as I am. He is rather too fond of painting, but I suppose it can't be helped.

6. Albert Campion

He is Margery Allingham's detective. In fact, he is another man who reminds me a bit of Uncle Felix. Campion is an adventurer, and quite probably a liar, and he has a pet jackdaw (which is a bird like a crow) called Autolycus. I like that.

5. Miss Marple

Miss Marple was created by Agatha Christie. She is a little old lady who lives in St Mary Mead. I was rather scornful of her at first, because she is so old and doesn't want to go anywhere or do anything, only sit and knit, but I do admit that I may have been wrong. In her own way Miss Marple is quite clever – she notices everything, but she manages to make people think that she doesn't see anything at all. I suppose she is actually rather like me. Only old.

4. Nancy Drew

Nancy Drew comes from America, and I like her very much. She is young, immensely clever, speaks French, can drive a motorboat, is an excellent shot, and understands psychology. She is also very rich, and she is always beautifully dressed.

3. Raffles

Raffles was created by an author called E. W. Hornung, who was the brother-in-law of Arthur Conan Doyle. He is rather like Holmes, in fact, but with one difference. He is a criminal. Hazel does not like Raffles because he is a thief. But that is *exactly* why I do like Raffles – because he sometimes commits the crimes, as well as solving them. It makes everything so mixed up and interesting. Raffles spends the day being very wealthy and playing cricket, and the night cracking safes with the help of his friend Bunny. I sometimes call Hazel Bunny, which she hates.

2. Hercule Poirot

He is Agatha Christie's most famous detective, and the best. He is Belgian, with big black moustaches and a round head. He looks like a caricature, and everyone laughs at him – until he unmasks the murderer every time. I like Poirot because he is dramatic and utterly brilliant. But I also like him because he does remind me rather a lot of Hazel Wong.

1. Sherlock Holmes

Absolutely the best detective in the world (apart from me), Sherlock Holmes was created by Arthur Conan Doyle. Holmes knows everything about everything, and he is interested in everything, just like me. He lives at 221b Baker Street with his best friend Watson (one day I would like to set up my own consulting detective agency and live there with Hazel), and they solve the most incredible crimes. Just like Hazel and I do!

THE BOOKS
THAT MADE
MURDER MOST
UNLADYLIKE

Robin Stevens here again! Hazel and Daisy have just told you about their favourite authors and books. Of course, they're very similar to mine – but not exactly the same. Did you know that in 1936, when Daisy and Hazel wrote this companion to their cases, Enid Blyton hadn't started her *Famous Five* series yet? Agatha Christie was still just a young author (by the end of her life she would have written over seventy novels), and one of my favourite crime writers, Josephine Tey, had only written her debut novel, *The Man in the Queue*.

So I thought I'd give you *my* list of favourite mysteries and mystery books, and explain just how they influenced my own stories. I love dropping hints into my books about my suggested reading list – see how many of the books here seem familiar to you!

Murder Most Unladylike

This book, and my series, began with two authors, Enid Blyton and Agatha Christie. I read and loved Blyton's *Malory Towers* books, as well as her *Famous Five* mysteries. I also loved Agatha Christie's mysteries – but when I started reading them, aged twelve, I struggled to find any characters who weren't adults. One of the only exceptions was her book *Cat Among the Pigeons*. It's set at a girls' boarding school, and the detective, Poirot, finds himself up against two brilliant schoolgirl sleuths called Jennifer and Julia.

There's a lot of Deepdean in *Cat Among the Pigeons*, but the book that really inspired the plot of *Murder Most Unladylike* is *Miss Pym Disposes* by Josephine Tey. It's set in a girls' sixth form, and someone is murdered . . . in the school gym. Beware: this book is *creepy*, so don't read it if you're one of the younger members of my Detective Society!

I couldn't mention *Miss Pym Disposes* in the book itself, but I did manage to slip in a reference to Josephine's earlier mystery *The Man in the Queue* (Daisy reads it at the very beginning). Daisy also reads *Peril at End House* by Agatha Christie and *Mystery Mile* by Margery Allingham. And I have Hazel reading *Swallows and Amazons* – it's not a mystery, but it is full of adventure and fun, and I loved it as a child!

Arsenic for Tea

This book is my country-house murder mystery, so when I wrote it I was thinking of Agatha Christie's *Sad Cypress*, as well as Ngaio Marsh's *Death and the Dancing Footman* (these books both take place in big country houses, and one of them has a rather deadly meal in it!). The Wellses are a little bit like the family in *Surfeit of Lampreys* by Ngaio Marsh (only a little – I think they changed as I wrote them!), and of course Uncle Felix is what would happen if you crossed Lord Peter Wimsey with James Bond.

But *Arsenic for Tea* was also inspired by a very *real* mystery, the Road Hill House Murder. This happened in 1860, and it was the first crime to be made properly famous in newspapers. If you want to know more about it, skip to the chapter on unsolved crimes! There is also a great (non-fiction) book about it called *The Suspicions of Mr Whicher* by Kate Summerscale, and the novels *The Moonstone* by Wilkie Collins and Dorothy Sayers' *Clouds of Witness* are based on it too. I'm so fascinated by this murder that I can't get it out of my head. It makes me sad and confused, and *that* makes me want to write about it again and again. In fact, I may very well use the Road Hill House Murder again in a future book . . .

And one last thing: I managed to sneak in a very small mention of one of my favourite detectives,

Raffles. He's a gentleman thief (so of course Daisy loves him) and he was created by E. W. Hornung. All his stories are online, so you can read about Raffles for free!

First Class Murder

This one's easy. It was based on Agatha Christie's *Murder on the Orient Express* – though of course it has a *very* different ending. It's a locked-room mystery, so I was also thinking of one of my favourite (non-book) mystery series, *Jonathan Creek*.

I did manage to slip a few reading references into *First Class Murder*. As well as *Murder on the Orient Express*, Daisy reads John Buchan's *The Thirty-Nine Steps*, and Alexander (my other bookworm character) mentions the totally brilliant *Trent's Last Case* by E. C. Bentley. Daisy and Hazel also use *The Baffle Book*, which is a real 1930s book of detective puzzles. These puzzles wouldn't make much sense to a reader today, but I still had a lot of fun reading them as research!

Oh, and if you've been wondering about the Junior Pinkertons, I promise you I didn't find *them* in a book. The Pinkerton Detective Agency was American, and totally real – they were Victorian, and so successful that at one point there were more Pinkertons than police in the USA!

Jolly Foul Play

The plot of this book came from two places. First was my favourite Sherlock Holmes story, *The Adventure of Charles Augustus Milverton*. It's about a horrid blackmailing man – and, of course, the horrid Head Girl in *Jolly Foul Play*, Elizabeth Hurst, is based on him. And the second . . . is *Mean Girls*. This classic film is about the sort of nasty gossip that spreads around a school, and how friends can turn on each other, and that was the other idea I needed to create *Jolly Foul Play*!

In this book the girls were really too busy to read, apart from letters, but if you're looking for an Agatha Christie to go with *Jolly Foul Play*, try *The Moving Finger* – it's all about nasty letters being spread around a village!

And finally a note on Inspector Priestley. He's Daisy and Hazel's favourite policeman, and this is the third case he helps the girls with. When I made up his name, I wanted it to sound a bit 'good' (priest-like!), but of course he also shares it with J. B. Priestley, the author of one of the best murder-mystery plays ever written. *An Inspector Calls* is so brilliantly creepy that I get chills just thinking about it (another one that younger Detective Society members should wait for). If only I could work out a way to get that plot into one of my books . . .

Mistletoe and Murder

In the first chapters of *Mistletoe and Murder* Daisy reads Dorothy Sayers' *Gaudy Night*, and that's because I used a lot of the ideas in it. Like Daisy, you may not get on with *Gaudy Night* if you're looking for a fast-paced murder mystery – I'd suggest waiting, just like with *Miss Pym Disposes*, though for very different reasons!

Of course it's a Christmas book, and so I was thinking of *Hercule Poirot's Christmas* and *The Adventure of the Christmas Pudding* by Agatha Christie. But in terms of plot, her book *Dumb Witness* is more relevant. (I didn't put a dog in *Mistletoe and Murder*, though I wish I had now!)

For Christmas, Daisy gets a set of Margery Allingham books, and Hazel gets Dickens (though I'd have bought her Wilkie Collins instead). They also open their presents in a scene that pays tribute to one of my favourite non-mysteries: *A Little Princess* by Frances Hodgson Burnett.

And finally, the cases that Daisy and George discuss are real (of course they are). The Maybrick case is a famous unsolved poisoning, and Franz Müller was accused of committing the first-ever murder on a British train. Did he do it? I'm not sure. Find out about some of my other favourite real-life cases in the Unsolved Mysteries section later – remember that real mysteries are rarely as tidy as made-up ones!

THE SECRET OF WESTON SCHOOL

The Junior Pinkertons' First Mystery.

Written by Alexander Arcady
(Junior Pinkertons co-President).

Weston Boys' School, Sunday 20th October 1935.

(Written in invisible ink, and decoded by Hazel Wong.)

This is George and Alexander's first case. Alexander wrote it out for me not long ago, and it's funny how similar it is to our own Deepdean cases, and yet how different. It's full of intrigue and danger and spying – I hope you enjoy it as much as I did!

– Hazel Wong

I

Dear Hazel,

I promised, ages ago, to tell you about some of the other mysteries the Junior Pinkertons have solved. Unlike you, we haven't come across any murders (the two of you have all the luck!), but we have had plenty of good cases all the same. This was our very first. I think it's brilliant, and I hope you will too.

It happened at our school, last fall. I guess it was about the same time as you and Daisy found that teacher of yours, Miss Bell, murdered. George and I were third years then too, and raring to find something to solve. We'd been reading my *Hardy Boys* and John Dixon Carr (do you know them? I can send a parcel to you if you like), so we were stuffed full of thoughts about smuggling and spies and night-time raids.

Which is why, when we heard what had happened to the post boy, we perked up our ears at once.

It was very early on Monday October 5th 1934. The post boy, whose name is Hanrahan, was in the lane that leads to the back gate of the Weston School walls, where all the tradesmen go, when a gang of roughs jumped out at him. There was a whole group of them, and they beat him awfully. They tore at his clothes, and pulled open his sack of letters and searched through them. But they didn't find what they were looking for – Hanrahan heard one shout, 'It's not here!' They threw the letters in the mud, and then ran off in a hurry when they heard the baker's boy, Thompson, coming. Poor Hanrahan was almost fainting when Thompson found him, though he was able to tell Thompson about the rough men. None had been wearing masks, but he did not recognize them.

As I said, that was on Monday morning. Once Thompson had called for help and someone had taken poor Hanrahan home, Thompson delivered that day's bread to the school kitchens. The news travelled from the kitchen maid to the school secretary, Ashby, who sorts and censors the letters – and soon the news was all around the school. George and I both heard about it at bunbreak because Ashby has favourites in the older years who hang about in his office, and they told their friends, who told their friends, and so it trickled down to us.

Then, on Monday night, the school library was broken into.

We heard of it on Tuesday morning, and this time we had it from our friend Bob Featherstonehaugh (you pronounce it like *Fanshaw*, Hazel – I didn't know that when I first arrived at Weston and I made an ass of myself), who was junior library monitor Bob told us that someone had kicked in the library door in the middle of the night and begun to pull books off the shelves. But the noise of the door being broken had roused Mr Holtz, the librarian, from his rooms in the masters' wing. He came down to investigate, and the vandal ran off before he could be caught. Then some of the other masters – Mr Miller, Mr Prince and Mr Gambino – ran to the library as well, thinking when they saw the scene that *Mr Holtz* was the vandal. Mr Holtz had to explain himself, and for a while was in a tight spot.

It made him so upset that he announced that he couldn't go back into the library, and so when the library monitors – Bob, who's the junior monitor, and the fifth year Inigo Bly, who is the senior monitor – arrived for their Tuesday morning duties, Mr Holtz told them they must clear everything away and take a thorough inventory to ensure that nothing had been stolen, only damaged.

'I think Holtz *was* the vandal, and is now trying to cover his tracks,' Bob said to us. 'He *said* he heard a noise, but who knows if that's true? Holtz seems like a good sort, but he is German, after all. I've been thinking for ages that he might very well be a spy.'

Bob's father does something frightfully important and secret in the Foreign Office, and as a result Bob is obsessed with stories about daring and bravery, fellows fighting off tigers or lions or anacondas, and finding jewels. Recently, because his father had been dealing with rather a lot of spies (we knew because Bob was always jawing on about this in lessons, and having to be shut up by Mr Miller or Mr Prince or Mr Gambino), he had also begun to read books about spies, and so now he was sure that everyone was one.

But Bob did not take an inventory of the books that Tuesday morning. Inigo Bly, the senior monitor, volunteered to do it all.

George and I didn't like Inigo Bly. He was one of Ashby's favourites, a slicked-back drawling fellow who always raised his eyebrows at you and made you feel foolish before you even opened your mouth. You know the sort. In fact, when I did open my mouth, he sneered and called me *Cowboy*, even though I've never been to the Wild West, Hazel, not even once (although I should like to), and he called George even worse things. I shan't tell you those.

Just like with that awful new Head Girl you've told me about, there wasn't anything to be *done* about Bly. He was two years older than us, and he was also a favourite of our Headmaster, Twining, as well as Ashby.

He made all of the younger boys slog for him (at Weston School, Hazel, the first, second and third years do chores for the fourth- and fifth-year boys, and it's called slogging). George and I had to tidy his dorm once, and it was foul.

But although Bob thought *Holtz* suspicious, George and I thought that *Bly's* behaviour was rather more so. Bly was certainly not someone who volunteered for a job if he thought one of the younger boys might do it for him. It seemed very strange to us that Bly would offer to tidy the library on his own, and not make Bob do it all. So after assembly we made our way to the ruined door of the library. I bent down and tied my shoelace, and George leaned casually against the wall. We both peered into the library.

And there was Bly. He was kneeling on the floor, books stacked around him. His face was drawn and serious, and he was writing in a little green leather book, propped open on his lap. Next to him I could see a small pile of folded papers.

Then he glanced up at the doorway and saw us.

'OUT!' he shouted. 'GET OUT!'

George and I leaped up and fled – and at that moment we both knew that something mysterious was going on at Weston School. We had found our first real case, and it involved Inigo Bly.

II

When George and I founded the Junior Pinkertons, we developed a very cunning way of holding meetings during cross-country races. We both start running very quickly (I can imagine you shivering, Hazel, but the fact is that it is important for detectives to be aerobic. I know that Daisy will agree with me), and then a mile into the course we veer off the track, scramble down a hill and duck into a little cave on the outskirts of the Weston School grounds. It even has a log in it, which is very handy for sitting on.

George is a faster runner than me, so he goes first (we knew that if we disappeared together, it would be far too noticeable). He was already sitting on the log when I arrived that Tuesday afternoon. We did the Pinkerton Handshake, and then I got out the Detective Box from its hiding place in a hollow bit of the log. The Detective Box used to be a biscuit tin, and it still has a Scottie dog on it. Sometimes I imagine that it is a real member of the Pinkertons. Imagine how many more crimes we could detect with a dog!

Inside the Detective Box were our puzzle books, some of George's gorier true crime stories, and my shorthand notebook and pen. These days, of course, there are all your letters to me too, and the ones I am partway through writing to you. I keep my supply of invisible ink in the box, and the log is where I sit and write. Once I have revealed the invisible ink on your letters, I have to keep them hidden, or I should be sent to detention for the rest of the year. You know even the dull covering messages we send each other sometimes arrive with holes and marks on them. I can't say how unfair it is that your school does not censor letters as heavily as ours does. Twining is such a fierce Headmaster. When he found a copy of the *rude* version of *The Arabian Nights* last term, he had it burned in front of all of us, and as I have said, nothing gets in or out of Weston without being read by Ashby first.

'Now,' said George. 'The post boy has been beaten, and the library has been broken into. Inigo Bly is behaving oddly. What does it all mean?'

I didn't know. I couldn't see how those things fitted – or if they did at all.

'Well, let's begin by writing down all of the facts,' said George.

We made a chronological list of all the things we knew, and then another list of deductions from the first list, and then I saw that, really, we had some rather good leads.

The Weston Mystery – What We Know

- The post boy was set upon on Monday morning by a group of people he did not know. Nothing was stolen from him.

- The library was broken into on Monday night by one or more people who ran away when Mr Holtz found them at it. Again, we have not heard that anything was stolen.
- The other masters thought initially that Mr Holtz was the thief, but they may be mistaken.
- Mr Holtz refused to clear up the mess himself, which Bob believes is suspicious.
- Inigo Bly volunteered to clear up, which we believe is suspicious.
- Inigo Bly was seen by the Pinkertons taking some sort of notes, a pile of papers next to him.

The Weston Mystery – What Does This Mean?

- The two attacks occurred close together. In the first case, the attackers did not find what they were looking for. Was the library attacked for the same reason? If so, then it's possible that, again, the attacker was startled before they could find what they wanted.
- Although the two attacks may be connected, they were most probably not committed by the same person for the following reasons. For the first attack, we are looking for more than one person. We are also looking for people who are *not* at Weston School, because it is hard for pupils to get out of the gates, which are almost always locked. More importantly, the post boy did not recognize his attackers, and he knows all of us at Weston. For the

second attack, we are looking for either one or more people who are at Weston School – boys, masters or servants – as it would have been impossible for anyone to get into the school building after the doors were locked last night. The school was also searched by the masters, after Holtz raised the alarm, and no one was found.

– We must find out what object or objects the thieves wanted from the post boy. And if someone was indeed looking for something in the library, were they after the same thing? Once we know this, we can work out who would have wanted to take it (or them), and why.

– Was Mr Holtz involved in the library break-in? We only have his word that he startled the vandal, instead of being the vandal himself – but if it was him, why would he refuse to go back into the library to tidy up, and so finish what he had begun at night?

– We must also consider Inigo Bly. Could he be the person who broke into the library? What was he doing when we saw him, and what were those papers next to him?

– We must try to search the library for clues (although Inigo may have got there before us).

– We should also speak to the post boy next time he returns to Weston School.

'If the two attacks are connected, what do you think the attackers were looking for?' I asked George. 'Jewels? Money? Blueprints!'

'Why would anyone be sending jewels or blueprints to Weston, or keeping them in Weston library?' asked George. I wish you could hear George, Hazel. He's so sarcastic. 'It can't be that. We must just detect, Alex. One of us must follow Bly, and the other Holtz. Shall we flip for it? I call heads on Bly.'

He took out a shilling, and spun it in the air. It fell down on the dirt floor of the cave. It was heads. Never flip a coin with George, Hazel. You'd think it was impossible, but I'm sure he cheats.

III

It's strange how good George is at tailing people. I have spent ages learning to slip from shadow to shadow, and keep out of sight, but George doesn't even try. Instead, he becomes more *there* than there. He knows that, because of the colour of his skin and his Indian surname, no one could ever not notice him, and so he uses that. He leans against a wall adjusting his cuffs or staring into a mirror at a fleck of dust on his shoulder, in the middle of the room but apparently completely uninterested in what anyone else is saying. I knew he would stay on Bly – so I went to find Holtz.

I thought he might be in the masters' quarters, so I tried to find him there. But it's really hard to go somewhere you shouldn't be at school. Everyone is liable to ask you what you are doing. In fact, it's jolly hard to tail anyone at all – which I know you know, Hazel. I kept on being turned away and having to go to lessons, and sit listening to masters droning on about deadly dull subjects with no excitement to them at all. I can't wait until I'm grown up and can become a real detective.

Then I tried the library. I stuck my head in – and there was Holtz. He was sitting at his desk, head in hands. He didn't look like someone with a secret. He just looked sad.

I came out of the library, passing some fourth years as I did, and ran into Ashby, the secretary. He's a tiny man with a big Adam's apple, and his suits always look just too big for him. He's so smarmy, Hazel, and usually he has a self-satisfied smirk on his face that is infuriating. But that day he looked rather pale. He was muttering something to himself, and looking at something in his hand, and he barely saw me at all.

But *I* saw *him*, and I saw what he was holding. It was the green notebook that had been on Bly's lap that morning.

I knew I had seen something very important. My heart was pounding. The bunbreak bell went, and I rushed to find George.

I found him near Bly, of course. Bly was eating his slice of seed cake, surrounded by other boys, his bad mood in the library seemingly gone. George was watching him, using the window to the science labs as a mirror to fix his hair. When he caught sight of me, George turned and came over.

I gasped out what I had seen in Ashby's hand. George did not look particularly surprised. It's a habit he has, and it's really annoying.

'It fits,' he said. 'Yes, it fits. It's a very cunning operation.'

'What is?' I asked.

'Well, listen to what *I* saw,' said George. 'You know what a cool customer Bly is usually? Well, he wasn't this morning. He went scurrying around Weston, carrying a pile of books and papers, going so fast that he kept on bumping into people. He'd go straight down the corridor towards a group of boys, and then thump into one of them. The boy would help him up and pat him down, and the two of them would talk for a moment before they both went on their way.

'I expect you can already guess what I should have seen at once, Alex. It took me until the third meeting to realize that there was something else going on. When Bly bumped into the boys, he'd push something into their hands.

'The next few times, with the fifth year Maskelyne and the fourth year Spackman, I saw what he was passing over. It was pieces of paper with writing on them.

The writing was different every time, so it wasn't crib notes or test cheats. Then, on the corner of one he gave to that fourth year, Van der Velde, I saw an address and I was certain. Bly was giving the boys *letters*. Alex, we must get back to the library and talk to Bob again. You keep him talking while I examine the books. I've a theory, and I must see if it's right.'

IV

Bob Featherstonehaugh was alone in the library when we arrived at lunch time. Mr Holtz had gone to ground in his office, to bind up some books, Bob explained (none had been taken, but several had been damaged, and Holtz was quite upset), and Bly was nowhere to be seen either.

I asked Bob for *Biggles: The Camels Are Coming*. I knew jolly well that it was on loan to Shepherd Minor, and I didn't particularly want it anyway – but I calculated that it would get Bob talking. It did. He chattered away about flying aces and daring missions, and I chattered back at him (you know how I can talk, Hazel – it's very useful, and quite unique among all these deadly silent English people), while George lounged against Bob's desk and flicked idly through the loan lists.

'Good grief,' he said. 'I'd never have pegged Van der Velde as a History buff. I thought he was more interested in Geography, since he follows that explorer father of his all around the world each hols. But here he is, taking out the sixth volume of Gibbon's *Decline and Fall of the Roman Empire* seven times this term. And look at these books taken out by Spackman and Maskelyne! They've kept mum about their study of Norse runes and Bornean tribes. How rum.'

Bob was halfway through a re-enactment of one of Biggles's greatest air battles. He didn't take a breath, or flinch at the boys' names, or the books George was mentioning. But they sparked something in my brain. Van der Velde, Spackman and Maskelyne were all boys who Bly had run into and handed papers to this morning.

Then George closed the loan book and winked at me. 'I think I shall just go and have a look at the shelves,' he said. 'Back in a tick.'

I was on tenterhooks waiting for him to return. I barely heard what Bob said. Then the bell rang. George rushed back up to the desk, seized my arm and frogmarched me towards History. Bob was just behind us, so although I was desperate to know what George had found, I had to make sure I was quiet about it.

'What did you find?' I asked George under my breath.

'Well,' he said. 'According to the loan list, the Gibbon isn't currently checked out, and ought to have been on its shelf – but it was missing, and so was *Norse Runes*. We know that Holtz is meticulous about library books being recorded properly, and would never wrongly record something as being checked out when it wasn't, and vice versa. That means we can safely assume that the Gibbon was one of the books damaged by the thief and taken away by Holtz for repair, so not yet returned to the shelf. Alex, I was almost sure before, and now I think I know.

'Remember those letters I saw Bly handing over. Let's assume that they were the papers we saw with him in the library earlier, and he was making notes about them in a little book. Then remember that *Ashby* had the book when you saw him, and also that Bly insisted on tidying up the library after it was broken into. Add to that the fact that some of the books damaged by the attacker were checked out again and again by the very same boys whom Bly handed letters to . . .'

'You think . . . it's *smuggling*,' I said slowly. 'Ashby and Bly are working together and . . . smuggling letters?'

It sounded like a plot in one of my books. But George nodded excitedly.

'Listen – this is what I think's been going on,' he said. 'We know that Ashby is the person who takes in all the letters, reads them and censors them. We also know that Bly and Ashby are friendly, and that Bly is senior library monitor. So – stop me if anything sounds wrong . . .

'What if boys are paying Ashby and Bly to make sure that their letters arrive uncensored? No one likes to think of their personal letters being read and tampered with, do they? So what if Ashby and Bly came up with a way for some boys to get around it? They give Bly money, Bly puts their names in his green book, gives it to Ashby, and Ashby separates out the letters addressed to those names when the post arrives each day. Then Ashby gives those letters to Bly, who slips them into certain library books.'

'Each boy must have been assigned a library book as part of the smuggling ring!' I said, understanding. 'It would be like . . . a spy's dead letter drop, right? A place they could use as their own special mail box. They'd take out any letters addressed to them and put their replies back in the same place to be smuggled out again the same way. That's why Bly wanted to go through the books on his own this morning!' I added. 'He wanted to make sure he got all of the letters out of the books before anyone else came snooping around.'

Now, Hazel, this was all very shocking. As I have told you before, Ashby reads every letter coming in or out of Weston. (That's why I always write you a neat and boring letter in ordinary ink, and on the back of my letters write what I actually want to say in invisible ink.) The idea that there was another way for letters to get in and out of Weston – and that Ashby was involved in it! – was really incredible.

'And that's why Bly was so upset this morning,' said George. 'He must have been panicking that someone knows about this scheme, and might expose it. Or, at least, that's what I think. But, Alex, here's the thing. *Bornean Tribes* was still on its shelf, and looked absolutely undamaged. So we can deduce from this . . .'

'That the attacker knew that there were letters in *some* of the books, but not exactly which ones!' I whispered. 'It rules out Bly and Ashby, seeing as they *did* know which books the letters were in!'

'*Precisely*,' said George.

'So the attacker – both times – is someone who *knows* about the smuggling but isn't part of it,' I whispered. 'Someone who's looking for a particular letter. But who? And why?'

It seemed to me that letters were running through this case. First the post boy had been attacked, and now we knew that the library had been secretly full of uncensored letters.

Just then, we passed Mr Prince in the corridor, scolding the fourth year Van der Velde for not handing in his prep for that week. 'I want it by tomorrow!' he said crossly, while Van der Velde hung his head.

'What if we talk to the post boy?' George asked, as we came into the classroom. 'We can do it tomorrow morning!'

'*Yes!*' I said, excited.

We stood as Mr Prince came in, and then sat again. In the row behind us Bob was jawing about his father's latest secret assignment. I was glad that he hadn't noticed George and me whispering together.

'Do be quiet, Bob,' said Mr Prince, sighing and scribbling something in his book. 'All right, third year worms. The Battle of Edge Hill. Who can tell me anything about it?'

While he talked, I thought. We had our case, only we didn't know everything yet. We knew that Inigo Bly was running a letter-smuggling business in the library. We knew that the post boy had been attacked while carrying letters. The villain had reach both inside and outside Weston School, and they were looking for a letter. But what the letter was, and why they were looking for it, we didn't know.

V

On Thursday morning George and I set our alarms for five a.m. under our pillows so that only we could hear them. We had been terribly worried that a servant would see us creeping downstairs, but no one stopped us. We slipped out of the tradesmen's door, and crouched down in the long grass beside the gates. We heard whistling coming along the lane, and then the post boy rang the bell on the gate. One of the maids hurried out to unlock the gate (we crouched lower in the grass), and then we waited. Two minutes later, the whistling came back our way, and we both stood up.

Hanrahan yelled in fright. He was still bandaged about the head, and looked rather pitiful.

George and I both hissed at him that it was quite all right, and we were not about to hurt him.

'Lads!' said Hanrahan, recognizing us. 'Twice in a week would have been too much. What d'you want?'

'We want to know what happened to you on Monday,' said George.

'You don't want to hear that!' said Hanrahan.

'But we do!' I said. 'It's so interesting!'

'Oh, all right, I'll tell you,' he said at once, as I knew he would. Hanrahan likes to talk even more than I do.

'Where exactly were you?' asked George. 'You must have been almost at Weston.'

'Well, I was,' said Hanrahan. 'But I'd turned back. Forgot a parcel from the greengrocer's that I'd promised Beryl.'

He turned red as he said that. Beryl is the prettiest of the maids.

'I knew I'd be late, but I didn't think anyone would mind – and that's when they jumped on me. I fought them off as best I could – I think I landed some good blows – and then Thompson got there.'

'So you were facing back towards Weston village? Not towards the school?' asked George quickly. We had thought that Hanrahan had already been to Weston when he was attacked, but now we knew that he hadn't.

Hanrahan frowned at him. 'I was,' he said. 'Why does that matter?'

But I knew why. My heart jumped, Hazel, for I knew then that the letter Hanrahan had been attacked for *was still in Weston School.* He had not reached the school before he was attacked, you see – which means he had not collected that morning's outgoing post. And if post is not collected, it goes back to Ashby. He would have handed the smuggled letters back to Bly, to keep in the library until they could be sent out again. That was why the library had been attacked that night. And then Bly had taken all the letters the next morning and handed them back to their writers – that's what we had seen. The letter must now be back with the boy who was trying to send it – but which boy?

124

VI

We came one step closer to discovering that when we crept back into school.

The fourth year Van der Velde had been caught out of his dorm in the middle of the night! He was walking through the masters' wing (which is illegal, and enough to get you in detention if you are caught), when he was attacked and knocked down the stairs by someone behind him.

He was found . . . by the librarian, Mr Holtz. Mr Holtz said that he had heard a noise outside his door, and stepped out to find poor Van der Velde lying on the floor. Van der Velde was taken to the San by Holtz and Mr Prince and bandaged up by the nurse. By the time we heard of the attack, he was awake, but he said he could remember nothing about what had happened. He told the nurse, and Headmaster Twining, that his mind was a blank about what had happened after he left his dorm. He had needed a glass of water, and he had got lost in the dark.

This was a very unlikely story. At Weston, the school and the dorms aren't separate places, like at Deepdean. There's just one enormous square building around a courtyard, with the classrooms in the middle, the boys' dorms in one wing and the masters' rooms in the other. But there was no reason for a boy to be out of his wing at

125

that time – and even less reason for him to be in the masters' wing.

I was also beginning to think that George and I had been wrong to dismiss Mr Holtz. He had now been involved in two of the three attacks: he had been the person to discover the library attack, and now he had been the first person to find Van der Velde. What if Mr Holtz *was* the person looking for the letter?

VII

The Junior Pinkertons held an emergency meeting on Thursday morning, as soon as we were let out for our run. It was raining, and the walls of our cave were cold and a little wet.

I had been thinking about Mr Holtz and Van der Velde, and I had a theory. 'What if we *are* looking for a spy?' I said to George, shivering. 'What if there's a *German spy at Weston School*?'

'You think old Holtz is taking information from Weston and passing it to Herr Hitler?' asked George. 'But he found out that someone – Van der Velde – knew, and was trying to send a letter out of Weston that would incriminate Holtz? So Holtz's been trying to find it, and now he's hurt Van der Velde?'

I nodded.

'Well, it's possible,' said George. 'Holtz had the opportunity. But, Alex, what about *Van der Velde*? We know that he bought into Ashby and Bly's smuggling operation, and we know that he's – well, not English. He spends all his hols travelling the world with his father. What if his *father* is the spy, and Van der Velde has been sending him information – and he's been trying to get hold of another boy's letter because he knows it's important? He might have just pretended to fall down the stairs too! Alex, we have to go and search Van der Velde's room while he's still in the San.'

'But Van der Velde is a fourth year!' I said. The fourth years' dorms are on the floor above ours – we usually don't have a reason to go near them.'

'Alex,' said George, winking at me. 'Don't you know who usually slogs for Van der Velde? Our friend Bob. And don't you know *exactly* what would make Bob swap with us, just for today? That new *Hardy Boys* adventure you've been hiding at the bottom of your tuck box.'

George really is excellent to have in a tight spot. He always thinks of something.

VIII

Bob wasn't sure about swapping at first – 'Van der Velde's all right,' he said to us, 'he lets me jaw on at him and never tells me to shut up' – but in the end the *Hardy Boys* book from Dad did the trick.

My heart was pounding again as we climbed the stairs to the fourth years' dorms. We were carrying cloths and a broom (George had the broom under his arm, like a field marshal's baton). I was sure someone would ask us why we were there instead of Bob. But all the boys we passed either ignored us or teased us for having to slog – no one was really curious at all. It's just as Daisy would say: if you *look* like you ought to be somewhere, people will simply assume that it is the truth.

George went striding into Van der Velde's empty dorm first. 'What a bore – we have to clean this whole dorm!' he announced loudly, and then he slammed the door shut.

As soon as the door was closed, we both leaped to it. I went digging through Van der Velde's bedding and trunk, while George roamed around the dorm, tugging on curtains and pulling open drawers. The room was terribly messy, and as I searched I got the uncomfortable feeling that we were not the first people to go through Van der Velde's things. Had Mr Holtz got there before us?

In the end it was George who made the discovery. He thumped the wardrobe in frustration – and a little knot of wood on it popped open. Inside it . . . was the letter!

It was in Van der Velde's handwriting, and there was no censor's mark anywhere on it.

'Read it!' I cried.

George pulled it open and frowned. 'It's in Dutch!' he said.

I gaped. What were we to do now?

'*Geachte Papa*,' said George. 'Um . . . *Dear Dad, I hope this finds you well. I am writing to you because—*'

'George,' I said. 'Can you *read* Dutch?'

'Near enough,' he said, frowning at the page again. 'It's not far off German really, and German's just a crosser sort of English with genders.'

I've never been more dumbfounded in my life. I stood there like an idiot while George read on.

'*. . . because there's something up at Weston. I'm sure of it. Mr Holtz—*'

'Hah!' I cried.

'Wait a bit,' said George. '*Mr Holtz has been . . . worried for a while, and I am too. Someone's been watching us, and going through our rooms. I've found my clothes folded in different ways, and a few weeks ago I lost one of your letters to me. It's happening to other boys as well. That* – hah – *that stupid Bob boy who's so bad at keeping his father's job secret, he's had things moved and taken, although of course he doesn't notice. I got him to tell me about it, when he thought we were just chatting.*

'Then, last week, Mr Prince confiscated a boy's letter during our History lesson – and it was one of the letters that come in through the secret method that I have told you about. I saw him realize that it was not marked by the censor, and I saw that he did not tell Headmaster Twining what he has found. I began to watch him, to understand why, and what I think is that he is the person who has been following me.

'He is very clever, and I think he knows that I have found him out. He seems always to be there when I turn round – I have not been into the library all week because of him, but I am writing this letter now and I will send it using the secret method tomorrow. Be careful and watch yourself too. I don't know what organization he is part of, but I think it must be hostile to us.

'All my love, Marc.'

'Golly,' I said to George. There was nothing else I could think to say. We had suspected Holtz and Van der Velde because they were foreign – but that was not the answer at all. I felt slightly ashamed of us for that, Hazel. *I'm* not English either, after all.

'Golly,' agreed George. 'I mean – *gosh*! It isn't Holtz or Van der Velde – it's Prince!'

I thought back. Prince was one of the masters who had been on the scene very quickly after the library raid. He also— Why, he *had* been writing something while Bob was talking about his father's exploits. He had helped take Van der Velde to the San after he was attacked, which means he must have been close by. George was right: Mr Prince was our spy!

What if Mr Prince had found out that Van der Velde suspected him – and had also found out that Van der Velde was planning to write to his father, to expose him? We had seen him speaking to Van der Velde, demanding something – what if it hadn't been prep after all, but *the letter*?

We pelted out of the dorm and back down the stairs. And there, in the oak-panelled front hall, we saw Mr Prince. He had his coat on, and his walking stick under his arm, and he was striding towards the front door.

'MR PRINCE!' we both shouted at once, and he paused just underneath the gold chandelier and looked up at us.

'Boys?' he said. 'What do you want?'

Then he saw the letter in George's hands.

I saw him see it, and the name Van der Velde on it, and realize what it meant.

'Why do you have that?' he asked. 'Come down here and give me that.'

'We shan't!' I said. I felt quite brave. But then Mr Prince came striding across the hall and up the stairs towards us, his face like thunder, and I felt much less brave.

'GIVE ME THAT!' he shouted.

'HEADMASTER TWINING!' I shouted. 'ANY-ONE! HELP!'

Mr Prince lunged at us. I threw myself at his chest, and George kicked his shins as hard as he could. I think he must have been surprised that we fought back, and that second of confusion was all we needed. He went down, yelling, and Headmaster Twining came round the corner, with Ashby rushing in front of him.

'WHAT is the meaning of this?' Headmaster Twining shouted at us.

'Mr Prince is a spy!' I panted. George and I have learned that although we are both just as clever as each other, it is better for me to speak if we want to be believed. 'He's been collecting information about boys and their fathers, and Van der Velde found out about it and tried to send a letter to his father to accuse Mr Prince, and that's why he was knocked down the stairs. And that's why the post boy was beaten too, and the library attacked – Mr Prince and his associates outside school were looking for the letter Van der Velde had written.'

It was not a very good explanation – but once we had shown Mr Twining Van der Velde's letter, and Mr Prince's room had been searched, there was no doubt about it. It was full of books with notes and plans and even sketches of things like ships. He was frogmarched away, and that was the end of that. Mr Prince was never seen at Weston again.

IX

We were expecting to find ourselves with medals, and a letter of thanks from the British Government for saving them from a German spy – but no letter came. Instead, one day we were called into Headmaster Twining's study to find a tall man with blond hair and a monocle standing there on the carpet.

'Boys,' he said. 'My name – well, you may call me M. You are to be congratulated on your enthusiasm. You solved your case very cleverly, and caught a spy. But I'm afraid there's a problem. This incident . . . you may have slightly misunderstood what is at stake. There are many German spies at large in our country at the moment, and because of that, it is important for our Government to keep an eye on both its own upper classes and those of Europe. The man you knew as Prince was part of that effort – on *our* side. He was sent by our Service to watch the boys and masters at Weston, but I'm afraid he took his mission much too far. The Hanrahan incident – which he ordered, using some really rather unsavoury types he'd met through a previous assignment – was deeply regrettable, as was the attack on young Van der

Velde. Prince was also tracking your librarian, to monitor him; of course, the man is quite innocent of any wrongdoing. Prince has been removed from his post. But our Service's effort will – must – continue. All I ask is that you keep silent about what I have told you, and that in future you do not let your detective missions interfere with our greater effort. Do you understand?'

'What?' said George. 'No!'

George is certainly the braver of the two of us. I didn't want to say anything.

'I believe I mis-spoke,' said the man, raising one eyebrow at him. 'You *must* understand and obey me, for your own good. So, do you?'

'We do,' I said at last. I trod on George's foot.

'Excellent,' said the man. 'And, by the way, I really do applaud you for your excellent investigative work. There is only one person I know who could match your wits – but never mind her. Perhaps it's a good thing you don't know each other.'

And you know, Hazel, it took me until very recently to realize it – but I think that girl might have been Daisy! And that man was – well, you know who he really is, and you know him better than I do. I only ever saw him once. That is why I am telling you this story now, and trusting that you will not pass it on further.

So that is the story of how George and I solved a case, and were mistaken, but everything still came right in the end. And, of course, that was only the beginning of our adventures . . . but those are stories for another time.

Love to you and Daisy,

Alexander Arcady

THE JUNIOR
PINKERTONS'
SECRET WORLD
OF SPIES

Hello, detectives. Alexander Arcady here. Hazel told me that she and Daisy were writing a companion to their case notes, and I asked her if I could contribute a chapter. She suggested this one (without telling Daisy), and I agreed. I'm not exactly a Detective Society member (I'm part of the Junior Pinkertons!), but I do know my stuff about spies: I helped Daisy and Hazel catch one on the Orient Express, and George and I have had some run-ins with them in our Junior Pinkerton cases as well, as you've just seen.

So, here goes.

First, here's a bit of recent British spy history. The British Secret Intelligence Service (that's the proper name for it, George says!) was set up at the beginning of this century because Britain was rather worried about Germany. They were convinced the Germans were spying on them, you see, and decided to get their own back (they were quite right, because of course what happened next was the Great War in 1914).

So the Secret Service Bureau was set up in 1909. Its leader was a man called Alfred Cummings. Cummings was a bit odd (he signed everything in green ink, for some reason), but he was a very hard worker, and he made his spies work very hard too. During the Great War, while ordinary soldiers were in the trenches, German and British spies were fighting a battle of wits as they raced to gather information (among spies it's called *intelligence*, by the way).

Once the Great War was over, the British Secret Intelligence Service stopped being worried about Germany and began to be worried about Russia. In 1917 they'd had a revolution and got rid of their monarchy (to the British, and to my Russian grandmother, this is a Bad Thing. But my American mother says that we Americans had one too, ages ago, and we're quite all right now. I don't know which one is right. I guess it's a confusing thing). So for a while everyone was afraid of the Bolsheviks (that's what the people who took over in Russia are called, and Grandmother has told me awful stories about them), and the British spied on them like anything. Now, of course, Britain is beginning to be worried about Germany again because of Herr Hitler. History really is just one thing after another.

*

So that's the history. But how do spies go about their work? Well, they know that sometimes you have to be very clever to pass information on safely. Here are some of the Junior Pinkertons' very favourite methods (George told me most of these, though I did know the lemon juice one already, of course!).

- In ancient Rome, messages were stuffed into the body of a hare, which was then given to a trusted servant in a hunting net to pass on to its intended recipient!
- In Elizabethan England, messages were often put inside waterproof boxes and then hidden in wine or beer bottles. Very small messages were also concealed in metal bullets.
- Greek generals (this is disgusting) used urine to write secret messages. If you covered the area with dust, you could read the message!
- Luckily, during the Great War, spies had started using lemon juice instead. This is how a lot of German double agents were caught, actually – men found with lemon juice in their rooms were immediately convicted and shot.
- Other places where spies have hidden messages include:

  A hollowed-out coin
  The base of a pipe

A wine cork
Board games
Playing cards

– And finally the most perfect way I have read about
    to hide messages (I do want one of these very much):
    the combustible notebook. These are fitted with a
    little pin, and when it's pulled out the notebook
    goes up in flames to stop anyone hostile reading it!

The best spies have always been people who other spies
would never suspect. For example, during the Great
War there was a network of spies called 'La Dame
Blanche'. (That means 'the White Lady'. This isn't
because they were all ladies, although quite a few of
them were. I told this to Hazel and she was pleased.)
They watched trains going in and out of German-
occupied Belgium. They couldn't work out how to get
this information back to the British – until they realized
that midwives were allowed to cross military borders.
The network smuggled their messages out of Belgium
wrapped around the whalebones in the midwives'
corsets!

Here are some more rather brilliant spies from
recent times. Most are people, just like the midwives,
who you would never suspect . . .

Mata Hari

Mata Hari was Dutch. Before the Great War she spent her time dancing without many clothes on (this is true, we aren't making it up). In 1916 she fell in love with a Russian man, and was caught by French soldiers on her way to see him. The soldiers told her that she could only keep on visiting him if she spied for France. So she did – but she didn't much like the French, so she decided to be clever. She became a double agent, passing the information she got after spending time with the French on to the Germans in exchange for money. Finally, though, the Germans turned on Mata Hari by sending a message using a code the French had already cracked; of course, this revealed her identity to the French. Poor Mata Hari was caught and shot by a firing squad. This seems a rough deal to us, when all she really wanted was to visit her boyfriend.

Sidney Reilly

Sidney Reilly was known as the Ace of Spies, which is a brilliant name. He spied for the British during the Great War after he got a job working for German shipbuilders. This allowed him to pass intelligence back to the British using German boats. Then, in 1918, he was sent to Russia to try to overthrow the Bolshevik government (remember, Britain didn't like them!). This failed, and in 1925 the Bolshevik government got their own back by luring Reilly over to Russia, where they put him in prison, questioned him, and finally executed him.

That's the story, anyway. But there are rumours that Reilly had become sympathetic to the Bolsheviks, and his death was actually faked . . .

Marthe Cnockaert

Marthe Cnockaert was a very clever spy. From what I've read about her, I think she must have been a little like Daisy. She was born in Belgium in 1892, and she worked in a German military hospital in occupied Belgium. She was so good at her work that she earned an Iron Cross from the Germans, but Marthe had actually been persuaded by a friend to work as a spy for the British. She used her role as a nurse to find out military information, and to try to defeat the Germans.

She was caught when she left her engraved watch behind during an expedition to lay explosives underneath a German ammunition store. (See? She was fearlessly brave.) She was caught and sentenced to life imprisonment in Belgium, but was released in 1918 when the Great War ended.

*

So there you go! That's the Junior Pinkertons' Guide to Spies and Spying. I'd love to be a spy when I grow up – either that or a codebreaker. George says be careful what you wish for, and I guess he's right, but I don't see why I shouldn't long for exciting things to happen, just like they did to the people in the stories we've told!

CODEBREAKING
WITH
HAZEL WONG

I do hope Daisy won't be too cross when she reads Alexander's section on spying, or the one by George later. I think they're both excellent, so I've decided that if she doesn't like it she will just have to lump it.

There's only one thing that could possibly follow Alexander's chapter, and that is something on codes and codebreaking. Simple codes have been used for thousands of years, in lots and lots of different languages. In fact, the earliest known cipher was from 1900 BC – almost four thousand years ago! – which was found in hieroglyphs in Ancient Egypt.

Alexander and I use very easy codes (as well as invisible ink) to write each other messages. Here are a few simple – and not so simple – codes that you can use to write to your friends and Detective Society members. All the answers to the questions I've set are given at the very back of the book – once you've done all the exercises, have a look to see if you're right!

Reversing words

This one is easy. All you need is a pen and paper, and a bit of brainwork! For example, the word 'backwards' backwards is: sdrawkcab.

Can you decipher this line? *Tip*: Decode each word separately, not the whole sentence at once.

Naedpeed loohcs rof slrig

Deepdean school for girls

Swapping letters

The simplest version of this code is made by taking a letter from the beginning of each word and putting it at the end. For example, the word 'swapping' would be 'wappings'. But you can make it more difficult to decode by moving two letters, or more. The word 'swapping' then becomes 'appingsw', and so on!

Pig Latin

This isn't actually a code, or Latin, or anything to do with pigs. It's simply a way to disguise what you are saying.

The rules of Pig Latin are very easy:

1. First you have to know the difference between vowels and consonants. Daisy says *everyone* knows this, but she is particularly clever, so if you don't, then the vowels are a, e, i, o and u, while consonants are all the other letters of the alphabet.

2. For words beginning with consonants, any letters before the first vowel are moved to the end of the word. Then 'ay' is added to it.

3. For words beginning with vowels, just add 'yay' to the end! Can you crack this line?

Ownay ouyay allyay ancay eakspay igpay atinlay!

Now you all can speak piglatin

Morse code

Morse code was invented in 1836 by a man named Samuel Morse. He was trying to show how messages could be sent as sounds along telegraph wires, which had never been done before. Before then, if you wanted a message delivered anywhere, someone would have to do it in person. But as soon as messages could be sent as electrical signals, they could travel much faster!

There are only two types of signal in Morse code: a short one and a long one. A short signal (it's called a dit,

but you can just say 'dot'), is shown by a dot like this: ·
A long signal (which is actually called a dah!) is shown
by a dash like this: –

The most famous Morse signal is SOS, which stands
for 'Save Our Souls'. It's what you send when you
want to call for help. An S is three dots in a row, and
an O is three dashes in a row. So SOS in Morse code
is: · · · / – – – / · · · (I've used a / to separate the
letters in the codes.)

Daisy and I used Morse code on our Orient Express
case. We did it by tapping sharply for each dot, and scrap-
ing our nails along the wall for a dash. It worked very well!

See if you can use the table below to figure out the
Morse messages on the next page.

Letter	Morse
A	· –
B	– · · ·
C	– · – ·
D	– · ·
E	·
F	· · – ·
G	– – ·
H	· · · ·
I	· ·

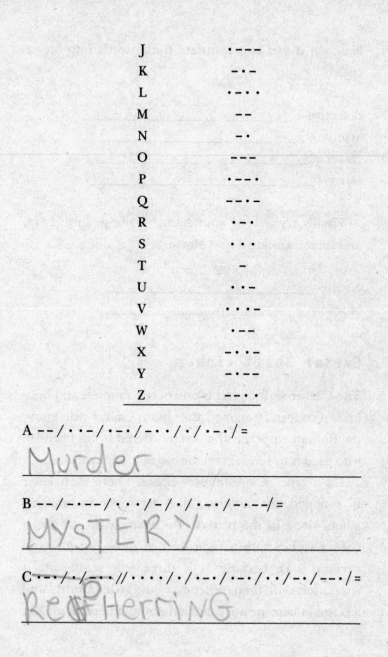

J	•‒‒‒
K	‒•‒
L	•‒••
M	‒‒
N	‒•
O	‒‒‒
P	•‒‒•
Q	‒‒•‒
R	•‒•
S	•••
T	‒
U	••‒
V	•••‒
W	•‒‒
X	‒••‒
Y	‒•‒‒
Z	‒‒••

A ‒‒ / ••‒ / •‒• / ‒•• / • / •‒• / =

Murder

B ‒‒ / ‒••‒ / ••• / ‒ / • / •‒• / ‒•‒‒ / =

MYSTERY

C ••‒• / • / ‒‒• / •••• / • / •‒• / •‒• / •• / ‒• / ‒‒‒ / =

Red Herring

Now see if you can translate these words into Morse code!

detective = _____

arsenic = _____

Hazel = _____

Daisy = _____

Finally try writing your name! Write it down here, and then translate it into Morse.

Name: _Anika_____

Morse: _•—/—•/••/—•—/•—/_____

Caesar shift cipher

The Caesar shift cipher is one of the simplest and best-known codes. It is named after Julius Caesar (you know, the Roman emperor who was murdered by his friends), who used it to send secret messages to his army.

It's a type of substitution cipher, where each letter is swapped for another, and it works by shifting letters along in the pattern. For example, if you had a Caesar cipher with a right shift of three, an A would become a D, because D is three letters after A. If it was a left shift, then the letters would go backwards, and a D would become an A (and an A would become an X!).

Here's a table that shows you a Caesar shift cipher with a right shift of three.

Normal:

A	B	C	D	E	F	G	H	I	J	K	L	M	N	O	P	Q	R	S	T	U	V	W	X	Y	Z

Cipher:

D	E	F	G	H	I	J	K	L	M	N	O	P	Q	R	S	T	U	V	W	X	Y	Z	A	B	C

Now try to work out what these words mean. They've been encrypted with a Caesar cipher with a right shift of three, like the table above. Look at the letters in the cipher row, and swap them with letters from the normal row.

FUXPSHWV = *CRUMPETS*

IRRWSULQWV = _____

FOXHV = _____

Now try and complete this cipher with a *left* shift of three! Some of them have already been done for you.

Normal:

A	B	C	D	E	F	G	H	I	J	K	L	M	N	O	P	Q	R	S	T	U	V	W	X	Y	Z

Cipher:

X	Y	Z	A	B	C	D	E	F	G	H	I	J	K	L	M	N	O	Q	R	S	T	U	V		W

All right. If you'd like a really *difficult* challenge, see if you can work out what these words are! You'll have to figure out what shift they are on your own (and no cheating!) . . .

Zntavslvat Tynff = _____

Mbylfiwe Bifgym = _____

Paroay Igkygx = _____

Transposition cipher

Now, a transposition cipher is extraordinarily clever. It involves characters being shifted around into different positions, rather than just changing letters. For example, if we put 'MURDER MOST UNLADYLIKE' into a transposition cipher, it might end up in a block like this, where you read downwards instead of from left to right:

M E S L L
U R T A I
R M U D K
D O N Y E

So you would send the message as: MESLL URTAI RMUDK DONYE. Then the person receiving the cipher would put it back into the block to decode it!

Can you work out what this says?

FTSR ICSD RLME SAUR

= _____

Now you can create your own transposition cipher, and play around with the number of rows and columns you put your sentence into. If you find you have spaces left in your grid, just use an X instead. This will then become part of your encrypted message, and make it even more difficult!

*

And now for something rather fiendish. See if you can crack the codes in the letter I wrote to Daisy on the next page. She got bored halfway through. I hope you can do better! (I have used a single / to mark where a letter ends and another begins, and a double // to mark a space between words.)

Dear Daisy,

I am writing you a letter in code, so that you can practise your codebreaking. dna hits emti ouy tsmnu't eugi pu efbreo oyu etg ot hte den, ecusbae I ehua meghtosni yreu rompitnat ot letl ouy. / [Morse code cipher section] /). I owknay ouyay idn'tday earhay operlypray, ecausebay ou'veyay eenbay ingtryay otay askyay emay estionsquay aboutyay ityay everyay incesay. zk nrj wifd dp wrkyui Cpfl xlujjuu kyrk) reu zk nrj rsflk dp xireuwrkyui Cz'd jliu pfl xlujjuu kyrk kff). qn ajb knnw ruu, jwm qn ajb mrnm, jwm cajc rb wxc j bnlanc xa j uhbcnah. tub won ym rehtaf stnaw em ot emoc emoh ot nruom mih − dna, ysiad, eh syas uoy dluohs emoc htiw em, os I t'now eb enola no eht yenruoj. / [Morse code cipher section] /

Say you will?
Hazel

Did you get everything right? To see, check the last pages of this book!

THE CASE OF THE DEEPDEAN VAMPIRE

Being an account of

The Case of Camilla Badescu,
an investigation by the Wells and Wong
Detective Society
(mainly Daisy Wells).

Written by Daisy Wells
(Detective Society President), aged 14.

Begun Thursday 21st November 1935.

Now it's time for another case! Daisy has written this one as well —
it's a mystery that confused me (and rather frightened me, if I'm being
honest). But it does prove that it's a good idea to read things that
are not just mystery stories — if it hadn't been for me and Dracula,
I'm not sure if we would ever have solved the problem!

— Hazel Wong

I

Of all the cases Hazel and I have investigated so far, the Case of the Deepdean Vampire was one of the strangest and most interesting. It was not a murder, which was a pity – but I did solve it very cleverly, as usual, and I am convinced that it ought to be written down properly, so that other people can read it one day and be impressed.

I asked Hazel to do it, but she is still busy writing up her notes for the Case of the Murder of Elizabeth Hurst, our Head Girl (that *was* a murder, and a very exciting one). However, I remembered how good I was at writing up the Case of the Blue Violet, and I realized that I could do it perfectly well myself. After all, I am not only an excellent detective but a truly first-class writer. I am the Honourable Daisy Wells, and I can do anything.

Now, I am sure that one day Daisy Wells will be recognized as the greatest consulting detective the world has ever known (the second greatest will be Hazel Wong, of course). However, I must admit that international fame has not quite happened to us yet. We are currently fourth formers at Deepdean School for Girls. I am the President of our Detective Society, and Hazel Wong is my Vice-President and Secretary. She is also my best friend, which I am glad about. Not that there was ever any danger that she was not, but all the same, I did spend the first part of this autumn term wondering.

The facts of the case are these. At breakfast on Thursday 21st November I was watching our new prefects try to keep the shrimps in order. (If you read Hazel's account of Elizabeth Hurst's murder when it is finished, you will understand why we have new prefects, and why I might be interested in them.) However, one of the most important things for a detective to remember is the principle of *constant vigilance*. You cannot simply think about one thing. You must watch and listen to several things at once. I am an excellent detective, and so I was keeping half an ear on the chatter at our fourth-form table. The others (Kitty, Beanie and Lavinia from our dorm, as well as Clementine from the other dorm) were talking their usual useless nonsense, but then something came through that made me sit up and take notice.

'And she climbed past our window like a lizard at two in the morning – *upside down!*' said Clementine

Delacroix. 'I was lying in bed awake, and I saw her. Our dorm is right below hers, you know. She must have come out of the window above us!'

Now, Clementine is a terrible gossip. Most of the things she says can be ignored, but all the same, this sounded most interesting.

'She did *not*!' said Kitty scornfully. Kitty is also a gossip, so she and Clementine often don't get on.

'I tell you, she did!' said Clementine. 'I saw it with my own eyes. I'm not surprised – I've been waiting for something like this to happen for weeks. You see, Camilla Badescu is a vampire.'

I keep close watch on everyone at Deepdean as a matter of course, and so I already knew quite a lot about the fifth former Camilla Badescu. She comes from Romania, and she is new this year – she went straight into the fifth form, which is unusual. She is tall and pale, with dark hair, and she is exceedingly haughty. She is rude to everyone, including the mistresses – everyone, that is, apart from her best friend, Amy Jessop. Camilla and Amy share a dorm with Eloise Delacroix (who happens to be Clementine's sister) and two other girls, and they have become as close as anything since a few weeks after Camilla arrived.

'Don't be silly,' said Kitty. 'People don't climb *upside down*. And anyway, there's no such thing as vampires.'

'Yes there is, Kitty Freebody, and Camilla is one,' said Clementine. 'She comes from Romania, doesn't she? Well, Romania is next to Transylvania, and everyone knows that's where vampires come from. It's perfectly obvious if you think about it. She never eats anything at dinner and her hair has one of those window's peaks—'

'*Widow's* peaks,' said Lavinia.

Clementine glared at her. 'And how would you know, Lavinia? Are you a vampire too?'

Lavinia bared her teeth. Clementine rolled her eyes.

Beanie, eating her toast, looked alarmed. 'You don't really mean it?' she asked.

'Of course I do,' said Clementine. 'I tell you, I know what I saw!'

Kitty soothed Beanie, and I glanced at Hazel, to see how she was taking things. She looked rather worried – Hazel doesn't enjoy ghost stories, and this sounded very much like a ghost story. But I was not quite so sure.

In my experience, people rarely *do* know what it is they saw. Their minds are dreadfully lazy, always playing tricks on them. But all the same, there is a reason behind everything – and I wondered what the explanation for this story was.

'Anyway, if you want proof that Camilla's a vampire, look at Amy Jessop,' Clementine went on. 'I know they're supposed to be friends, but look how pale and thin she's got since Camilla arrived in her dorm! My sister Eloise says that Amy's even begun to sleepwalk. That's why I was lying awake last night. I can sometimes hear the floor in their dorm creaking above our ceiling, and I thought I might hear her doing it.'

'Fourth form!' said the prefect on duty, turning to us suddenly. 'Eat up your breakfasts before the bell rings!'

We went silent and ate. I ate very quickly, to give myself more time to think. Most people are slow to do anything, which is foolish. If you do all the boring things in life like meals and prep and getting dressed extremely quickly, you have more time to detect.

Once I had finished my toast, I thought about Camilla and Amy. It was true that they seemed to have become close very quickly – and that was odd. Amy herself is known for being very polite, and good at lessons – her essay on *Macbeth* even won a prize at the beginning of this term, and was featured in quite a prominent paper. Camilla, as I have already explained, is stand-offish and rude – that Amy had picked *her* to be friends with was unusual. Amy had lost other friends because of it – she and Camilla spent almost all their time together now. I had noticed this, but I had not enquired further. I saw that I must do so now. Vampires are not real, but all the same, people don't simply imagine someone climbing past them, out of a window. I wanted to know what Camilla was really doing, and why.

II

On the way down to school from House after breakfast, I told Hazel that I thought I might have found the Detective Society a new case.

'You don't think she *is* a vampire, do you?' Hazel asked anxiously, and I knew I had been right: she did think it was a ghost story.

'Of course not!' I said. 'But I do believe that Clementine saw Camilla climbing out of the window, and I want to know *why*.'

I made sure that Hazel and I walked just behind Camilla. That morning she was walking with Amy, as she always did. They had their arms linked, and they were walking slowly. Amy was hunched over, her head almost drooping against Camilla's shoulder. I saw what Clementine meant – she looked unwell, quite weak. I also observed Camilla. She too was pale, and there were hollows under her eyes. She looked like someone who had not slept much the night before. Clementine's story was standing up so far.

We could observe our subjects – but of course, because we were only fourth formers and they were fifth, we couldn't simply go up and quiz them. We had to simply watch. I looked closer – and this time I saw something on Amy's neck. It was half hidden by her school collar, but it looked like a scratch – or a cut. I nudged Hazel, and she saw where I was pointing at once. We hung back, to let them get ahead of us, and then I turned to face Hazel.

'That mark, on her neck!' said Hazel. 'You know that's where vampires bite their victims?'

'Hazel!' I said to her. 'That was a cut, not a bite! You know as well as I do that there are no such things as vampires.'

'But – an unusual mark on the neck *is* one of the signs,' said Hazel. She said it rather nervously. Hazel really is terribly silly about the supernatural.

'All right, Hazel,' I said. 'Explain to me. What makes someone a vampire?'

I don't bother much with stories where nothing is real. Murder mysteries and spy books are all right, and so are books with names and dates and facts, but novels where people come back from the dead are not. I realized that I didn't know much about vampires – but Hazel would.

'Their powers only work properly at night, they drink blood, they can turn into anything they like – bats or rats or a pillar of mist – but they can't go anywhere without being invited, garlic and silver make them ill, they can crawl down walls like lizards, and if they drink your blood you'll become a vampire too,' said Hazel without drawing breath.

'Really, Hazel,' I said. 'You do read rubbish. But thank you.'

'I do not!' said Hazel. 'Anyway, it came in useful just now, didn't it?'

Really, Hazel has become very bold this term. Anyone would think she was becoming her own person. I tried to look severe, and keep us focused on the case.

'Listen. You saw Amy just now. She looks miserable – but so does Camilla. If she was a vampire, preying on Amy, wouldn't she be more smug? Now, let's put out feelers this morning. By the end of the day I want to know everything there is to know about Camilla – and Amy, while we're at it. And I want you to remember that there are *no* such things as vampires.'

III

I am always prepared to uncover new information at Deepdean. I have threads carefully set up, and all I need to do is tug them to put them in motion.

At bunbreak Hazel and I went over to see the third formers. 'What do you know about Camilla?' I asked. They are a very rude, bold year, and so nothing but a direct approach will do.

'She's a vampire,' said Binny Freebody immediately. 'She drinks Amy Jessop's blood. She's got a dark power over her.'

'You are stupid,' I said, because it is not good for Binny to be told she is anything else. 'That's a fairy tale!'

'It's *true*,' said Binny, widening her eyes. She really is unsquashable, even after the events of this term. 'I've heard three different people say so. Anyway, look at them! Amy never goes anywhere without her.'

I looked over at Amy and Camilla, sitting together on a bench. Amy was pinched and pale, a pretty contraband floral brooch pinned to the collar of her Deepdean blazer the only flash of colour anywhere about her. She was drooping worse than ever, and Camilla was whispering in her ear. Camilla had very red lips, I noticed, and her teeth were slightly pointed.

Hazel shuddered. 'Come on, Watson!' I said, nudging her. 'Buck up! These third formers can't help. Let's go and talk to Violet.'

Violet Darby is one of the Big Girls. Hazel and I did her a favour during the Case of the Blue Violet a few months ago, so she is in our debt.

That morning, as usual, she was sitting on a wall by herself, writing a letter. I motioned to Hazel, and approached her.

'Good morning, Violet!' I said.

169

Violet jumped. 'Daisy!' she said. 'Hazel. Are you all right?'

'Perfectly,' I said. 'But – Violet, we're worried. It's Amy. We think there's something wrong with her.'

Violet is soft-hearted, and just as I had hoped, she wrinkled her brow at that, and sighed. 'You've noticed?' she asked.

'Of course we have,' I said. '*All* the younger girls have.'

I nudged Hazel, who I knew was blushing. She is still annoyingly bad at espionage.

'Camilla's a bad influence,' said Violet. 'Amy oughtn't to have become friends with her. But she's too caring. She's had to look after her mother her whole life – her father went missing at the end of the war, you see, which usually means *died*, and Mrs Jessop never recovered from it. Amy didn't even get to meet him – it's awfully tragic. Anyway, I suppose she thought Camilla needed looking after too – a new girl arriving from another country, knowing not a single person at Deepdean. But it's Amy who needs looking after now, if you ask me. She's not eating enough, and she looks so upset all the time. Camilla won't let anyone else come near Amy these days. She frightens them away! I've tried to help, but what can I do?'

'What happened to make them friends?' asked Hazel. She is interested in this sort of thing – I suspect it reminds her of the time when I decided to befriend her.

'Oh, I don't know,' said Violet. 'They simply began hanging about together – walking to the sports field and school and things. Perhaps it was being in a dorm together, or perhaps they discovered they had something in common?'

I was wondering what on earth Camilla Badescu could have in common with Amy Jessop when suddenly there was a commotion behind us in the quad. Hazel and I turned round. Violet stood up with a start.

Amy had slumped back in a faint on the bench. Camilla was leaning over her, eyebrows drawn together fiercely, clutching Amy's hands, and on Amy's neck was a streak of red.

'She's hurt herself!' cried Violet. 'Oh dear!'

Several people ran for Mrs Minn – but Camilla and Amy stayed frozen in their places.

Hazel seized my arm, and I began to have an uncomfortable feeling about this case.

IV

'The same thing happened in *Dracula*,' said Hazel, in our dorm at lunch time. 'Lucy Westenra had a mark on her neck that wouldn't go away, because Dracula kept drinking blood from it. And she was pale, and weak, and sleepwalked – just like Amy.'

Reports from the San had come through via a third former. Amy was not badly hurt – but the cut on her neck we had observed that morning had opened up again.

'Don't be a chump, Hazel,' I said. I refused to call her Watson when she was being so silly. 'If Camilla had been biting Amy in the middle of the quad during bunbreak, someone would have noticed. *Dracula* is a book. Think about the *facts*. What are they?'

'Amy has a cut on her neck, she isn't eating properly and she is sleepwalking,' said Hazel reluctantly. 'Camilla is being protective of Amy; she is going everywhere with her and she has been seen climbing out of a window at night.'

'Exactly!' I said. 'Now, what does *that* sound like? Why, it sounds as though Amy and Camilla have a secret. And we must keep on detecting until we discover what it is!'

V

I was determined to keep vampires out of the case – but that evening we got ourselves mixed up with the spirit realm again in the most frustrating way. After

Prep we all went to the common room. The wind was whistling against the glass, and Beanie shivered. 'It sounds horrid out there,' she said, making her eyes very wide.

'You're such a baby, Beans,' said Kitty, putting her arm around her shoulders.

'I think we should tell ghost stories,' said Lavinia.

I knew perfectly well that Lavinia only wanted to tease Beanie, and I waited for Hazel to excuse us so that we could go and detect. But—

'Oh, yes, let's!' said Hazel.

I pursed my lips at her, asking what on earth she thought she was doing, but she ignored me even though she must have known perfectly well what I meant.

Kitty told a story about a doll that got closer and closer to a girl's bed until it killed her (I assumed that the real murderer was moving it, to disguise what was going on – that was how I would have solved the case, if anyone had asked me), and then Lavinia told a story about something awful scratching on the door of a house (a specially trained dog, of course, meant to terrify the inhabitants so that they would run away and leave the house empty), and made Beanie cry.

'I hate ghost stories!' she sniffed.

'You're a baby,' said Lavinia. 'I haven't even *started* on all the Deepdean stories. There's that shrimp who drowned in the pond, and the mistress who starved herself to death in the music rooms. And then there's that man who's been prowling around the sports fields.'

'It's true,' said Clementine, who had been listening in to everyone's stories. 'He's huge and hairy, and if he catches you he'll do away with you.'

'Next you'll be saying he's a werewolf!' said Kitty scornfully, and Beanie began to cry again.

'There really *is* a man,' said Clementine forcefully. 'I've seen him. But, look – none of this is a patch on Amy and Camilla.'

'Not again,' grumbled Lavinia.

'It's *true*!' hissed Clementine. 'Camilla's a vampire! Don't just take *my* word for it. Wait until I tell you what Eloise heard last night. She told me about it at lunch today.

'She woke up because Amy sleeps in the bed next to hers. She was tossing and turning, muttering things – things about being watched. She kept saying *Go away*. That made Eloise sit up, and then she saw the *truly* awful thing. There was a figure at the head of Amy's bed, looming over her in the dark. *Camilla!* Eloise called out – she didn't know what to do – and Camilla came over to her. Eloise says that she *floated* across the dorm like a ghost. She stood over Eloise's bed and held out her hands, just as though she was about to choke Eloise. Eloise must have fainted then – and she woke up this morning feeling dreadfully weak. It was as though something had been taken from her in the night. Her memory – *or her blood*!'

'If Camilla took her memory, how could Eloise tell you the story?' asked Kitty scornfully.

'Well, who knows, with vampires?' asked Clementine. 'Anyway, that must have been when Camilla climbed out of the window – probably to hunt for more victims! I'm lucky to be alive, really I am.'

'*We're* not!' said Lavinia, making a horrid face at Clementine. 'Anyway, I don't believe it.' But she was frowning, which I knew meant that she was afraid. Clementine's story was rather alarming – or at least it would have been, if I had believed in ghost stories.

But then I glanced at Hazel to see if she was upset, and I saw that although she was pale, she looked pleased. I suddenly understood what she had done by encouraging the stories. Just in the same way as I used a Ouija board last year to help solve the case of the murder of Miss Bell, Hazel had been hoping that the ghost stories would come round to Camilla – and, indeed, they had. We had heard more facts in the case. Despite myself, I was rather impressed with my Watson.

VI

Now, I am excellent at keeping myself awake – it is one of my most useful detective talents. It proved particularly useful on this case. Over the next week we kept watch on Camilla and Amy's dorm. By *we*, I mean *me* – Hazel is *not* excellent at keeping herself awake. She believes she is, and then she falls asleep over her casebook, snoring so peacefully that I see no point in waking her.

I observed Amy sleepwalking twice – both times she was caught by Camilla, and dragged back into the dorm. They continued to appear very tired, and both only picked at their food. Amy's cut did not heal, and her fingers strayed to it often.

'Daisy!' said Hazel on Tuesday morning. 'Are you all right?'

'I'm perfectly excellent!' I said, blinking. 'Why?'

'You put the butter knife in your tea,' said Hazel. 'I think your strange night existence is telling on you.' Then she laughed, as though she had made a joke. I glared at her. Of course, she was wrong. I could have carried on for as long as I liked – but I was lucky. The event I had been waiting for occurred the following night – exactly a week after Clementine had first seen Camilla climbing.

As usual, I stayed awake until everyone else in the dorm was asleep, and then, at one o'clock precisely – I looked at my watch – I got up, climbed out of bed and leaned over Hazel.

'Watson,' I whispered. 'It is time to detect.'

Hazel opened her eyes with a snort. She really has much to learn about subtlety still.

Now, Camilla and Amy's dorm is on the other side of House, above the other fourth-form dorm, so we had to pad along very carefully so as not to make any sound. I took Hazel's hand – she does tend to stand on noisy floorboards if she is not directed properly – and we crept together down the corridor and up the stairs to the door of the fifth-form dorm. Just to the left of it is a large bay window that was perfect for our purposes. Its long curtains blew in the breeze – Matron likes to keep windows open at all times, for our health – and they hid us perfectly, while still giving us a view of both the window to the fifth-form dorm, and its door.

We both tucked ourselves in by the window, and settled down to wait. I concentrated on House, the noises it made – and that was why I noticed what was happening before Hazel did.

Out of the dorm window came a figure. It was dark-haired, wrapped in a long dark cloak. It came out headfirst, and there was a moment when I thought it was about to climb upside down – but then it turned, and began to shimmy hand over hand down the drainpipe. I saw immediately how Clementine, squinting through the darkness – or anyone else not watching as carefully as I was now – might *think* that they had seen someone climb facing downwards. Camilla's hair was as dark as her clothes, and the wind blew her cloak upwards, hiding her pale face – but although she climbed well (not as well as I can), she climbed in the usual way.

I knew at once what course of action to take. 'Let's follow her!' I whispered to Hazel. 'We *must* know where she is going!' Sometimes detecting is all about deduction, and that is perfectly interesting, but sometimes it is about action, and I do have to say that I prefer the action.

'You go!' said Hazel. 'I'll wait here – in case Amy sleepwalks.'

At any other time I might have argued, but the moment was already slipping away. I had to give chase.

I threw up the window, scrambled onto the window-sill, reached out and took hold of the pipe, and just like that I was on my way. I looked up and saw Hazel's face, pale and concerned, and then she was gone, and I was on the hunt.

Naturally I had ensured that I was wearing my darkest dressing gown, and had shoes on. It is always important to be prepared for all eventualities, so I had no real difficulties keeping myself concealed. The only moment's concern I had was when I reached the ground outside House, and could not at first see which way my target had gone.

Then I caught a flash of movement at the edge of the lawn, heading towards the path down to school, and I was in pursuit again. I kept to the trees, in the shadows (I have practised this skill, and was very pleased to be using it at last), and flitted after Camilla just as though I were a ghost. It was excellently done, and I almost wished she would notice.

She didn't. In fact, she seemed most distracted. I could really have been walking five paces behind her, and she would not have seen me. She was constantly patting something in her pocket, and I deduced that it must be very important to her. She didn't seem to feel the cold, and walked through the night without a shiver.

But where was she going? Her steps faltered by the gate to the sports field. She paused – she turned – and in that moment I knew what Camilla and Amy's secret was.

Camilla walked across the hockey pitch and stood in the centre, waiting. I had to hang back by the gate, for there is no cover on the fields, apart from the pavilion and the tall oak tree. And out from behind the tree itself came another figure.

My eyes were used to the dark, and I saw with perfect ease that it was a man with shaggy hair and a ragged beard. His clothes were old and torn – he was one of those men who are everywhere on the roads, tramping from place to place. He raised his left arm, and I saw that his right was only a stump.

'Give it over,' he said to Camilla.

'Here,' she said, taking her hand out of her pocket. I saw that she was holding money, in shilling notes – I could not tell exactly how much, but from the crackle it must have been several pounds. 'Now won't you go away?'

'Where else would I go? Not to her mother,' said the man desperately. 'Look at me! I'm a monster. She won't want to see me.'

'But you're destroying Amy!' said Camilla.

'Well, I've been destroyed as well,' said the man, raising the stump of his arm. 'I'm sorry, but there's nothing else to be done. I have nowhere else to go.'

Camilla made a hissing noise, and then she spun round and stormed away, out of the gates. She passed me without noticing a thing.

Now I was alone – alone with Amy's father. For, of course, he could not be anyone else. I saw the chain of events in my head quite perfectly. He had not died after all. I had heard about men like him – who had been broken by the war, and did not want to go back to their lives. Perhaps he had even run away from his post, and been too ashamed to go back home. So he had stayed away from Amy and Mrs Jessop, and let them believe he was dead – until he came across Amy's essay in the newspaper. It would have told him that she was at Deepdean, and so he had come to see if he could get money from her. He must have been utterly desperate – I could see from his ragged clothes that he must be homeless now, with not enough to eat.

Of course, he was the werewolf man Clementine had told the story about. He must have hung about on the sports fields, waiting for his chance to speak to Amy and demand money from her. Amy was used to looking after her mother, Violet had told us so – she would want to protect her from the truth about her husband, and would have agreed to get the money to him.

And that first time they met, at the beginning of term – Camilla must have been walking with Amy. She had become part of the secret, protecting Amy just as Amy was protecting her mother, and that was why she and Amy were friends.

Amy was looking pale and ill because she was afraid of what might happen if she did not keep on paying her father. That was what her sleep-talking had meant: she did not want *Camilla* to leave her alone, but her father. And, of course, Camilla's behaviour was explained as well. She was not cross and secretive and creeping because she was turning Amy into a vampire, but because she was trying to help her. She climbed out of House every Wednesday night (and it was always Wednesdays, I realized) to give him the money, to save Amy from having to do it. Even the cut on Amy's neck made sense. She had cut herself on something – her brooch, perhaps – and in her distress she had worried at the wound until it opened again. Camilla had been holding her wrists at bunbreak to stop her making it any worse.

I thought all this out at once, but then I was faced with a rather more difficult problem. What ought I to do, now that I understood the story? There was a blackmailer who must be stopped – but he was also a man who must be sent home, where he belonged. Perhaps I have been around Hazel too long, but I knew that she would expect me to do more than simply turn about and come home.

I pondered (very quickly, the way I do everything), and then I saw what I must do. Ghosts, werewolves and vampires are made up – but people believe in them. Perhaps I could use that. I remembered what Eloise had said, too, about Camilla gliding across the floor – of course, Deepdean nightdresses are pale grey, and in mine, and my dark shoes, I would look just as much like a ghost as Camilla had.

Still in the shadows of the gates, I slipped off my dressing gown and wrapped it about my head, so that my face was covered. The clouds had been scudding past the moon, but now there was a break in them and the whole field was bathed in a ghostly light. I took my chance.

I glided out of the shadows and moved forward, my feet twinkling just as though I were dancing.

I saw Amy's father catch sight of me. He started, and turned. It was time for the second part of my plan.

'Jessop!' I cried, making my voice very loud. 'JESSOP! I SEE YOUR WICKED SOUL! WHY DO YOU TORMENT YOUR FAMILY?'

'Who are you?' gasped Mr Jessop.

I paused. 'I AM YOUR CONSCIENCE!' I cried.

'No!' he shouted. 'No!'

'Why have you become so cruuuuuuuel, Jessop?' I asked, trying to talk the way ghosts do in stories.

'I – I have to! I need money!' gasped Mr Jessop. 'Everything's been taken away from me! I can't get a job, and I can't go home – what if Connie won't have me back after what I've done? I ran away from my regiment! I cracked up!'

'Of course she'll have you back!' I said. I had rather stopped being a ghost, but I could tell that the spell had already worked. 'Once you love someone, you don't care at all about how they look, or how they behave, or the things they've done. People are dreadfully stupid, but there it is. Connie will forgive you if you go back to her properly, and explain yourself. And stop asking your daughter for money! It's all backwards, and not very nice.'

'I will!' Mr Jessop cried. 'I promise!'

'Good!' I said. 'And if you don't, I shall haunt you at night until you die.'

It was a very silly touch, but it did the trick. Mr Jessop turned and ran.

I waited until he was gone, and then I unwound the dressing gown from my head and took a deep breath. I felt that I had done rather well. I had solved the mystery *and* helped Amy Jessop. Even Hazel could not fault me.

VII

I got back to a House in chaos. Amy had sleepwalked again, and Matron had caught her at it – and then caught Camilla as she climbed back in through the window. I crept in under cover of the shouts, and found Hazel lurking in the second-floor corridor.

'Did you find out anything?' she asked.

'Yes!' I said. 'I know everything, Hazel. I've solved the case!'

And I told her. She was impressed – but she wouldn't let me tell Amy and Camilla what I had done. Apparently, although I thought I had done well, I had been rather teasing to a man who was down on his luck, and it was not nice to gloat.

I was rather cross at first about that, because it would have been terribly useful to have been owed a favour from more fifth formers, but I do have to admit that Hazel understands people far better than I do. I let it go.

'Aren't people funny?' Hazel asked thoughtfully. 'The ones you think are the worst are really the nicest. Camilla was being a good friend, and we all thought she was wicked. It's a bit like Lavinia, I suppose. Or—'

'Don't say Clementine,' I said. 'She really *is* horrid.'

'I was going to say *you*,' said Hazel. 'Don't look like that! I don't mean you're horrid. I mean – you're not the way I thought you'd be when I first met you.'

'I'm sorry to have disappointed you,' I said.

'Oh no,' said Hazel. 'I like the real you much better.'

I looked at her suspiciously, and thought how glad I am that Hazel is my best friend. She knows far too much about me to be anything but.

'Hazel,' I said. 'I have an idea. Camilla being a vampire was just a rumour – but I think we ought to spread a rumour of our own.'

VIII

The next morning I spoke to several people – just a few words, nothing more. There is an art to such things. By the morning after that it was well known all around the school that Camilla Badescu was a princess. *That* was why she was so haughty, and why she could not sleep or eat – because she feared assassins coming for her in the night. Amy Jessop was in on the secret, and that was why *she* had been so beside herself. Suddenly everyone looked at Camilla with the sort of awe that comes from a title – and they looked at Amy kindly, because she had cared so much for her friend. It was a little backwards, but it was close enough.

The next Monday morning brought a letter for Amy. She opened it at lunch, and we watched her. She gasped – she turned red and white – and then she began to cry in happy confusion. Camilla rushed over to her, looked at the words on the page, and then threw her arms around Amy.

'What is it?' cried Kitty.

'I'll find out!' said Clementine, and she went marching over to Eloise. She was back three minutes later with all the details. Amy's father, Mr Jessop, was back. It seemed he had hit his head just before the end of the war, and only remembered who he was a few months ago. He was broken, inside and out, and seemed to have been tramping for a long while, but now he was home, and Mrs Jessop had welcomed him. It seemed that Mr Jessop's fears had not been realized, and nor had Amy's. Mrs Jessop did not need to be protected after all. Hazel looked delighted, and I realized that I was as well.

IX

Today is Wednesday again, and I have just finished writing all this up. It does take a while – perhaps I understand now what Hazel means when she tells me she is busy with her case notes. I am sitting on the wall beside the lawn, eating my bun, and Camilla and Amy have just walked by arm in arm. They were laughing at something Eloise had said, and there was colour in both their cheeks. I am pleased to have proved that there really are no such things as vampires, and I am quite ready for our next case. Who knows what we might find when we arrive in Cambridge for the holidays?

GEORGE'S GUIDE TO UNSOLVED MYSTERIES

My name is George Mukherjee, Co-President of the Junior Pinkertons, Weston School's most brilliant detective agency. When Alex and I are on a case, we always get our man, and so do our friends in the Detective Society. But other detectives are not so acute. Whenever things are a bit slow with our own cases, I like to exercise my brain by thinking about some fascinating unsolved cases from history. I believe that I have already solved quite a few of them – see what you think about the following problems . . .

Jack the Ripper

This is one of the most famous unsolved cases in British history, and the most gruesome.

Between August and November 1888 five poor women were brutally murdered in the foggy, muddy streets of London. They were all killed in very similar ways, at night, and in the dangerous Whitechapel area of the city.

The police (who were not very organized at that time, and did not know how to properly investigate the scene of a crime) couldn't work out who the murderer was – and then (this is where it becomes really fascinating) the killer began to tease them. He wrote them a letter telling them they would never catch him, and signed it 'Jack the Ripper'. Some people think that the letter was a hoax – but whether or not it was, Jack the Ripper got away with it. He was never caught, and no one has ever been able to agree on who might have killed those ladies.

The police first thought that a man called George Chapman, a hairdresser in Whitechapel, might have committed the crimes. He did work nearby (and he was a Polish migrant, which made the police more suspicious of him. This is an unfair thing that often happens during investigations, because no English person wants to believe that another Englishman could do awful things). But Chapman was probably not guilty of the Ripper murders, although he *did* poison several of his wives. The methods are not the same, and so I believe he should be ruled out.

Then the police and the public thought it might be a famous actor called Richard Mansfield. He was acting in a play called *Jekyll and Hyde*, from a book written by Robert Louis Stevenson. It's all about a man called Jekyll who creates a villainous alter ego for himself called Hyde, who likes to go rampaging through London, murdering and causing chaos. The play was closed after the murders began – but it took Mansfield a long time to persuade people that he only *played* a murderer on stage.

There is one more explanation that I think is far more probable. From the way they were murdered, it's likely that the murderer was a doctor or surgeon. The body of a doctor, Montague John Druitt, was found floating in the Thames soon after the last murder. Could he have been Jack? We will never know for sure . . . but I think it makes perfect sense.

The Cheapside Hoard

This is almost as fascinating, if not as horrid. In 1912 a group of workmen were excavating a cellar on Cheapside Road in London. As they dug, one of them noticed something glinting in the ground – they had discovered an old wooden casket full to bursting with jewels, gems and other precious objects. There were around five hundred pieces of treasure, including a carving of Elizabeth I, an exquisite gold watch set with a massive Colombian emerald, and sapphires, diamonds and rubies from India and Sri Lanka. The jewels were all from the sixteenth and seventeenth centuries – which proves that the British have a very long history of taking things from other countries in the world and keeping them as their own.

What is interesting about this hoard, and what Alex and I keep on talking about, is that *no one knows who put it there.*

It might have been hidden by a jeweller or a wealthy gentleman fleeing the English Civil War. But why didn't they come back for it? Did they forget where they had buried it? Did they die before they could tell anyone where it was?

Some of the jewels must have been smuggled into England, possibly by pirates (you see why we think this is such an exciting story). There was a famous Dutch gem dealer named Gerrard Pulman who looted crates of jewels from Persia to sell in England. But on the way back to London the ship's surgeon poisoned Gerrard and threw his body overboard. The crates arrived in London half empty, and it's possible that some of Gerrard's stolen jewels ended up in the hoard. But who put them there?

The Pimlico Mystery

This is a marvellous Victorian murder mystery. I spoke to Daisy about it last Christmas hols, and we agree that we are both quite fascinated by it and the Maybrick case. It took place in an ordinary middle-class London house . . . but as you will see, the people in it were not ordinary at all.

Edwin Bartlett was a wealthy grocer. Adelaide Blanche de la Tremoille was his younger, French-born wife, and the Reverend George Dyson (another George, but not a bit like me, as you will see!) was the minister from the couple's local church.

Edwin and Adelaide were married in 1875. They met Reverend Dyson ten years later, and he became a close friend of the couple. In fact, they liked him so much that Edwin named him the executor of his will. This means that, if Edwin died, George would be the person responsible for sorting out all his money.

Then Edwin fell ill. Edwin and Adelaide's marriage hadn't been happy for a while. Now she began to rather fancy Reverend Dyson, and some witnesses say that her husband *encouraged* her to do this.

On to the murder . . .

On New Year's Eve 1885 Edwin went to sleep next to his wife in their Pimlico flat. The next morning he was dead. When he was examined, his stomach was found to be filled with liquid chloroform.

Chloroform is the colourless, sweet-smelling liquid that people use to knock each other out in Alex's spy stories. But in large doses it's fatal. Where had it come from? Well, the Reverend had been to four different pharmacies in the weeks before Edwin's death to buy small amounts of chloroform (this was so he could avoid signing the poison book, the place where you have to record any large purchase of poisons – highly suspicious behaviour). And he said he had done that because Adelaide had asked him to buy chloroform for Edwin. She claimed that it had been prescribed by his doctor (small amounts can have medicinal value). But what this confirms to me is that George and Adelaide were working together to bump off Edwin . . .

The odd and extraordinary thing, and the reason why this murder is so mysterious, is that no one has ever been able to understand *how* the chloroform got into Edwin's stomach. There was no evidence of burns in the throat, which you would usually expect. Experts were baffled, and because of the fact that they could not explain *how* Adelaide and Reverend Dyson had committed the crime, they were never convicted.

It's quite obvious why they *wanted* to murder Edwin, though. Edwin's original will stated that Adelaide could only have his money if she didn't remarry – but he changed his mind about that only four months before his death. Might Reverend Dyson, as executor of the will, have made this change so that he and Adelaide could get Edwin's money? It seems very likely . . .

The Road Hill House Murder

This is another Victorian murder mystery that is very famous, and very sad. Now that I know Daisy, I keep imagining it taking place at her house, Fallingford. I know that a murder *did* happen there, so perhaps that's why.

On the evening of 29th June 1860, Samuel Kent locked up his family home, Road Hill House. In the house with him were his servants, his children from both his first and his second marriages, his second wife and (most importantly) their little son, Francis.

No one heard anyone breaking in, but in the morning Francis's nursemaid, Elizabeth Gough, woke up and discovered that Francis was missing, and there was a downstairs window open. The family and neighbours searched everywhere – and finally Francis was found in the outhouse, dead.

The police were called in, and then a Scotland Yard detective called Mr Whicher. He ordered a search of the house, which uncovered a bloody nightgown hidden up a chimney. The nightgown was simple and plain, and so it was first thought that it might be Elizabeth's. There was a theory that she and Samuel Kent had been in love, and the nursemaid had killed Francis because he'd discovered their affair. This really does seem unlikely, as Francis was only three, so not very interested in grown-up affairs.

But then Mr Whicher found another suspect – Constance Kent. She was Samuel's daughter from his first marriage. She was not treated well by her stepmother (she made her wear plain clothes, like the servants), and she resented her half-brothers and -sisters, especially the favourite, Francis. Constance was strong enough to have killed Francis, and she was missing one of her nightdresses . . .

Mr Whicher accused her, and everyone was outraged. She was wealthy and English – once again no one liked the idea that someone who *seemed* nice could commit such an awful crime. Her trial collapsed, and no one else was ever accused. But years later, Constance confessed to the murder. Was she being truthful? I believe she was.

The Eilean Moore Lighthouse

This mystery is rather creepy. Hazel does not like me talking about it, but it is so fascinating that I can't leave it out.

Eilean Moore is a tiny island in the Outer Hebrides (small islands off the north coast of Scotland). It's empty apart from a lighthouse and the people who keep it, so that it stays lit to guide ships through the night.

On 26th December 1900 Captain James Harvey was sailing a ship carrying the replacement lighthouse keeper, Joseph Moore, over to the island. They were expected, but all the same there was no welcome party waiting when the ship docked. Surprised, the captain sent up a warning flare to remind the lighthouse keepers of his presence.

There was no reply.

Joseph Moore made his way along the cliff path towards the lighthouse – but when he got there, *no one was to be found*. There should have been three people in the lighthouse, but it was empty. Odder still, only two coats were missing from their pegs, the kitchen contained half-eaten meals and a chair was overturned. Oh, and the clock had stopped. It looked as though the lighthouse keepers had left in a hurry. But why would one of them run off without his coat?

Moore and the captain searched everywhere on the island, but the missing men were nowhere to be found. Their log entries make for interesting reading, though. On 12th December Thomas Marshall, one of the lighthouse assistants, wrote that there were 'severe winds the likes of which I have never seen before in twenty years'. He also noted that James Ducat, the principal lighthouse keeper, was 'very quiet' and that the other assistant, William McArthur, was praying. In later entries, all three men were praying. As seasoned sailors, none of the three should have been afraid of a storm. And which storm were they afraid of, anyway?

199

There were no storms in the area on that day – nothing was reported until several days later.

The final log entry was made on 15th December. It simply read: 'Storm ended, sea calm. God is over all.' No one knows what is meant by that last sentence, and no one knows what happened to the men – no bodies have ever been found. Could they have been abducted? (But there was no one there to abduct them.) Attacked? Washed out to sea during a spontaneous walk along the cliffs? (But why did one of them leave his coat?) Or (sorry, Hazel) were darker forces at work?

I do not know the answer – but I do wonder. Was the storm a real one, or was it man-made – I mean, were the three arguing; an argument that had a deadly ending?

The Disappearance of Agatha Christie

This, unlike the Eilean Moore puzzle, is one of Hazel's favourite mysteries. It is one that left the police and the public completely baffled. But, all the same, we think we may have quite a good idea as to what really happened . . .

On the evening of Friday 3rd December 1926 the writer was at the country estate she shared with her husband, Archie. She went upstairs to kiss her daughter goodnight, and then, at 9:45 p.m., she took the car and drove away from the house. Her car was found abandoned near the Silent Pool, a nearby natural spring – the site of the death of a young girl and her brother many years ago – but Agatha Christie was nowhere to be found.

Lots of people worried that Agatha Christie had chosen this as a place to kill herself. Others wondered whether she might have been murdered by her husband. You see, Mr and Mrs Christie had a very unhappy marriage, and Agatha had just discovered that Archie was having an affair, which she was very upset about. Had Archie killed Agatha to shut her up? One other suggestion was that the whole thing was just a publicity stunt – a way for Agatha to get her name in the papers and sell more books.

She was missing for eleven days, and the country was in turmoil. Her face appeared in the papers, and there were many pleas for information as to her whereabouts.

On 14th December she was spotted in a hotel in Harrogate, hundreds of miles from where she had last been seen. She was alone, and she was using the name Theresa Neele. She claimed that she had amnesia, and didn't know who she really was until she was discovered. But this doesn't seem likely to me. Archie Christie's mistress's name was Nancy Neele, and so *Theresa Neele* seems like a sly dig at Nancy and Archie.

My suspicions are that Agatha knew perfectly well who she was, and where – but after she found out about Archie's affair she decided she needed some time to herself. So she ran away, and used all her abilities as a creator of mysteries to do it very successfully.

CREAM BUNS
AND CRIME

It's Robin again! As you know, I believe that every detective mission should be full of bunbreaks as well as danger. When I'm not writing, I'm usually baking, and so I wanted to share some of my favourite recipes for *Murder Most Unladylike*-themed treats with you.

Please remember to be careful when you're using large knives and hot ovens – if in doubt, ask a nearby grown-up for help!

Mooncakes

Hazel is sent these cakes by her mother in *Murder Most Unladylike*. They're a taste of home: in Hong Kong she and her family eat them every year as part of the mid-autumn festival. They're made of sweet, slightly crumbly pastry, usually with strong-tasting lotus paste or red bean paste inside them, and sometimes salted duck's eggs as well.

Unfortunately, mooncakes, like most Chinese treats, are so difficult to make that my Chinese friends and I would recommend that you just go out and buy them!

Tang Yuan

If you really would like to try to make your own Hong Kong bunbreak, though, then here's a recipe for tang yuan. These are rice balls in a sweet soup that are traditionally eaten during Chinese New Year. Because they snuggle together in their bowl, they've become a symbol of family closeness – so as you eat these, think of Hazel and her family! But please, as this recipe involves boiling water, don't make it without the help of a grown-up. It's very easy otherwise, although you will probably need to go to a specialist grocery store to find all the ingredients.

Ingredients
  For the tang yuan:
  150g glutinous rice flour (you'll need to go to a specialist Chinese supermarket – but it'll be worth it!)
  2 tsp (teaspoons) caster sugar
  125ml water
  Red, green and yellow food colouring

For the sweet soup:

300ml water

75g brown sugar

2 pandan leaves (again, you'll need to find a Chinese supermarket)

75g ginger (the root, not the powder – peel it carefully and knock it about a bit to bruise it)

Method

1. In a bowl, mix together the rice flour and the caster sugar. Add water gradually (you won't need all of it, so be careful!) and knead with your hands until the dough is soft and smooth – not too dry but not too sticky either.

2. Divide the dough into three balls, and add a few drops of food colouring to each so that they are different colours. Knead each ball again, separately, until the colour has worked through the dough.

3. Split the dough balls into lots of even-sized mini-balls, just a bit bigger than a £2 coin.

4. Boil a large pan of water (this is where your grown-up steps in) and put the dough balls in for about 15 minutes, until they float to the surface of the water.

5. Have your grown-up take your dough balls (tang yuan) out of the boiling water and put them

in a bowl of room-temperature water to keep moist.

6. Now get your grown-up to put all of your sweet soup ingredients into another pan and bring them to a boil, then simmer until the sugar has dissolved.

7. Put the tang yuan in a serving bowl, pour over the sweet soup very carefully and eat!

Walnut Cake

In *Murder Most Unladylike* Hazel is also sent a Fortnum's walnut cake by her father – it becomes part of the dorm's midnight feast (and of the seance the girls hold afterwards). Hazel's cake, of course, is bought, but you can make your own version very easily at home!

Ingredients
150g butter
200g caster sugar
1 tsp vanilla extract
3 medium eggs
200g flour
2 tsp baking powder
½ tsp salt
2 tbsp (tablespoons) milk
100g chopped walnuts (buy them chopped, or ask a handy grown-up to chop them for you)

For the buttercream icing:
300g icing sugar
150g butter (softened)
2 tbsp milk

Method
1. Preheat the oven to 180°C/Gas Mark 4.

2. Cream the butter, caster sugar and vanilla extract in a bowl, and then beat in the eggs one at a time (the mixture may take a while to come together – don't worry!).

3. Sift together the flour, baking powder and salt, then add to the eggy butter-and-caster-sugar mixture. Then gradually stir in the milk.

4. Add the chopped walnuts and mix everything together.

5. Put the mixture into a greased and floured cake tin (20cm in diameter) and bake for 25–35 minutes.

6. Once it's baked, leave to sit out of the oven for five minutes and then turn it out of its tin (use your handy grown-up to help with this tricky bit) on to a cooling rack.

7. For the buttercream icing, put the icing sugar into a bowl and add the butter. Mix slowly at first, until it is basically combined (I have never yet found a way to do this without getting icing sugar all over the kitchen), and then whisk faster, with an electric mixer, if you have one. Finally add in the milk until the icing is thick but spreadable.

8. Wait until your cake has cooled and then cover its top and sides with icing. Decorate with walnuts.

Squashed Fly Biscuits

These are Daisy's favourite biscuit, and a regular at Deepdean bunbreaks (you'll find them mentioned in *Murder Most Unladylike* and *Jolly Foul Play*!). 'Squashed fly' biscuits are much less alarming than they sound – they're just raisin, or Garibaldi, biscuits.

Ingredients
    100g butter
    100g caster sugar
    250g self-raising flour
    1 medium egg yolk
    3 tbsp milk
    90g currants and/or raisins

You will also need a biscuit cutter or palette knife.

Method
    1. Preheat the oven to 180°C/Gas Mark 4.
    2. Cream the butter and sugar together in a bowl.
    3. Add the flour and mix again.
    4. Separate your egg! This is a tough manoeuvre – basically, you need to crack it in half over a bowl and let the clear stuff (the white) fall into the bowl, while you keep the yolk caught in the egg-shell. If you're struggling, ask a grown-up to help.

5. Stir the yolk into the mixture, but keep the white in the separate bowl.

6. Add the milk and stir again until the mixture forms a dough.

7. Roll the dough out on a floured surface until thin (about as thick as a pound coin) and then cut it in half.

8. On one of the halves sprinkle the currants and/or raisins evenly over the dough. Place the other half of the dough over the top and roll out again.

9. Get your biscuit cutter or your palette knife and cut out your shapes. As you want rectangular biscuits, a palette knife is probably easier!

10. Brush the biscuits with your egg white (if you don't have a proper brush, just use a clean paper towel) and sprinkle some sugar over them.

11. Place on a baking tray lined with non-stick paper and bake for 10–12 minutes until golden.

12. Place on a cooling rack. Once they are cooled they are ready to eat!

Coconut Macaroons

These macaroons aren't the beautifully coloured almond circles that you see in every pâtisserie window these days. These are delicious, hedgehog-shaped lumps of desiccated coconut and sugar that melt in your mouth and go all over your jumper. I first heard about them in the *Famous Five* books, and when I came to write *Arsenic for Tea*, I knew I had to give some to Daisy and Hazel. Mrs Doherty makes them at Fallingford, and I think her recipe would have been a little like this . . .

Ingredients

   2 egg whites
   100g caster sugar
   1 tsp vanilla extract
   120g desiccated coconut

Method

1. Preheat the oven to 180°C/Gas Mark 4.
2. Carefully whisk the egg whites (separate them from their yolks the way I told you in the Squashed Fly Biscuit recipe above) in a bowl until they form soft peaks: so that when you lift the whisk out of the bowl, you get solid peaks of white fluff. You can do this with a hand whisk, but an electric one is much easier. But

make sure you have a grown-up nearby when you use it!

3. Add in the sugar and vanilla extract and stir lightly.

4. Add the desiccated coconut and mix gently until it's all combined.

5. Spoon the mixture into small mounds (the size of a heaped tablespoon) on a baking tray lined with non-stick paper.

6. Cook for 15–18 minutes until golden brown.

7. Place the macaroons on a cooling rack.

8. Eat!

Jam Tarts

Jam tarts were on the menu at Fallingford too, at Daisy's birthday tea. This recipe is incredibly easy and fun – I love blueberry jam in mine, but I know that Daisy would prefer more traditional raspberry or strawberry!

Ingredients
    250g flour
    ½ tsp salt
    2 tsp caster sugar
    100g butter
    3 tbsp water
    A jar of your favourite jam

Method
    1. Sift the flour, salt and sugar into a bowl and rub the butter into the mixture with your fingers until it looks a bit like fine breadcrumbs.
    2. Stir in the water, one tablespoon at a time, until it forms a dough.
    3. Wrap the dough in cling film and leave it in the fridge for 15–20 minutes.
    4. Preheat the oven to 180°C/Gas Mark 4.
    5. Roll the dough out on a floured surface. Using a glass or tumbler or biscuit cutter, cut the dough into circles.

6. Place the dough circles in the cups of a greased and floured cupcake tray. Poke each little circle with a fork a few times, and then put a heaped teaspoon of jam into the centre of each one. (You don't have to use all the jam in the jar, of course! Keep some for your breakfast.)

7. Bake the tarts in the oven for 15–20 minutes until they are golden brown.

8. Take them out of the oven, cool them on a rack and then eat. Remember that it is NOT a good idea to try these before they are cool, because the jam goes molten hot!

Chocolate Cake

This is as close as I can get to Daisy's birthday cake! For maximum authenticity you need to pipe *Happy Birthday Daisy* on it with some extra white icing – but of course, you don't have to!

Ingredients

For the cake:
150g butter
150g caster sugar
3 medium eggs
150g self-raising flour
50g cocoa powder
1 tsp vanilla extract
Water

For the buttercream icing:
300g icing sugar
40g cocoa powder (sifted)
150g butter (softened)
2 tbsp milk

For the cream in the middle:
300g whipping cream
1 tbsp icing sugar
½ tsp vanilla extract

Method

1. Preheat the oven to 180°C/Gas Mark 4.
2. Cream the butter and sugar in a bowl.
3. Add the eggs and mix, then add the flour, cocoa powder and vanilla extract and mix again.
4. Finally add the water.
5. Spoon the mixture into a greased cake tin (20cm in diameter) and bake for 25–30 minutes.
6. Leave the cake on a wire rack to cool.
7. To make the icing, put the icing sugar and cocoa powder in a bowl and add the butter. Mix slowly at first, until it is basically combined, and then whisk faster, with an electric mixer if you have one. Finally add in the milk, until the icing is thick but spreadable.
8. Cut the cake in half horizontally (please get a grown-up to do this!).
9. Whisk the whipping cream – preferably with an electric whisk (again, use a grown-up) – and then stir in the icing sugar and vanilla (don't do this while you are whisking!). Spoon the whipped cream into the middle of the cake, and ice the top and sides with your buttercream.
10. Eat!

First-Class Fudge

Fudge is what Hetty, Daisy's maid (and honorary Detective Society member), brings Daisy and Hazel at the beginning of their Orient Express adventure. Fudge is absolutely delicious and the sweetest treat imaginable.

You need to have a grown-up present when you make this recipe. Hot fudge is something you do NOT want to get on yourself – stay safe, detectives!

Ingredients
1 tin/400g evaporated milk
120g butter
500g caster sugar
A clear cup full of cold water
2 tsp vanilla extract

Method
1. Grease a square cake tin (20cm in diameter).
2. Put the evaporated milk, butter and caster sugar in a heavy-based saucepan.
3. Get your grown-up to stir the saucepan constantly while it heats (this is boring, so you're lucky you don't have to do it!) until the sugar has dissolved and the butter has melted.

4. Bring to the boil and keep stirring. Boil for 20 minutes, stirring often. Be VERY careful as the mixture is VERY hot.

5. Spoon out a little bit of the mixture and drop it into the cup of cold water. This is the brilliant part: if you've done this right, it should form a soft ball at the bottom of the cup. If it doesn't, keep stirring the mixture and try again in a few minutes' time.

6. When it has reached the soft ball stage, remove the saucepan from the heat. Mix in the vanilla extract.

7. Have your grown-up stir the fudge until it starts to set.

8. Pour the mixture into the greased tin and leave to set.

9. Once it has set, cut the fudge into chunks and enjoy!

Mistletoe and Murder Mince Pies

I love Christmas so much that I wrote a whole book about it. Hazel and Daisy's adventure in Cambridge was one of my favourite stories to write – and, of course, it's full of descriptions of my favourite festive treats: mince pies.

This is my own special recipe. It's incredibly easy, but there is one thing that you MUST do: buy cupcake cases to bake your mince pies in. Otherwise you will have a Christmas bunbreak disaster!

Ingredients

280g or a jar of mincemeat (don't worry, there is no meat in this! It's candied fruit that you can buy from any store. Robertson's brand is quite nice.)

100g dried cranberries

1 tsp ground cinnamon

Zest of ½ orange (this means using a grater to scrape the outside of an orange into a bowl; make sure you don't get the white pith too!)

350g plain flour

100g caster sugar

225g cold diced butter

Cupcake cases

1 beaten egg

Caster sugar for dusting

Method

1. Preheat the oven to 180°C/Gas Mark 4.
2. Empty the jar of mincemeat into a bowl, add the dried cranberries, cinnamon and orange zest and mix. Put to one side.
3. Put your flour and sugar in another bowl, mix and then rub in the butter. Knead until the mixture comes together in your hands as a soft crumbly dough.
4. Line a cupcake or bun tin with cases.
5. Split the dough in two. Divide each half into 12 equal balls, and put 12 of the balls into the bottom of the cupcake cases. Press the dough balls out until they look like little tart cases with sides and a base.
6. Spoon some mincemeat mixture into each base, and then squash the other 12 balls of dough out flat, like little lids, and press them down on top of each tart.
7. Brush the tops of each pie with beaten egg, and then sprinkle caster sugar over them.
8. Bake in the oven for 20–25 minutes, until golden.
9. Cool and then eat! These are not the prettiest pies you've ever seen, but they are the tastiest!

Delicious Death

And finally a little note on the darker side of bunbreak. Yes, cakes and sweets are delicious, but in both history and in books they're also often deadly.

Have you ever heard of the Victorian poisoner Christiana Edmunds, who got so cross with her ex-boyfriend that she tried to kill him with boxes of chocolates laced with the poison strychnine?

Did you know that the Russian royal family tried to kill the famous monk Rasputin by throwing him a party and giving him cake containing enough cyanide to kill three grown men? The murder attempt failed, so they threw him in a frozen river instead.

And do you remember the cake in *Peter Pan*? The Lost Boys are told never to eat cake with green sugar on it, which doesn't seem to make much sense until you realize that when *Peter Pan*'s author, J. M. Barrie, was a child himself, bright green colours were made by using dyes . . . with arsenic in them.

There's plenty of deadly bunbreaks in Agatha Christie's books too. She even wrote a short story about a chocolate-box poisoning (I think she might have known about Christiana Edmunds as well). Her most famous cake, though, appears in the book *A Murder is Announced*. One of the characters is given a chocolate cake for her birthday. It's named 'Delicious Death' for its incredible richness, but, because this is an Agatha Christie book, the name soon becomes more literal . . .

THE MYSTERY OF THE MISSING BUNBREAK

As told by Rebecca Martineau, also
known as Beanie, aged 14.

Christmas 1935

Daisy and I spent last Christmas in Cambridge with Daisy's brother Bertie and the Junior Pinkertons, George and Alexander. What happened to us is recorded in my red casebook, and you may read about it any time you like. But mysterious things also happened to Kitty and Beanie while we were away, and they have finally been written down here . . .

— Hazel Wong

I

22nd December

It is snowing again. It has been snowing for what seems like hours and hours. It snowed on the train that took me and my best friend, Kitty, and her little sister, Binny, to London. I sat next to the window with my face pressed against the glass, drawing snowflakes in my breath with one finger, while Binny tried to get the lady with the fox-fur stole sitting opposite us to give her tuppence for a bar of chocolate. Binny, as Kitty is always saying, is a horror. I listened to Kitty and Binny argue while I thought about our other friends, Daisy and Hazel, on a train of their own, probably eating their sandwiches too soon. I missed them.

We had all left Deepdean School this morning. Matron waved us off at the station. Kitty and Binny were excited, but I wasn't. I hate the end of term. It always makes me feel sad. Our dorm's final midnight feast was the night before last, and even though we had mince pies sent by the father of our other dorm mate, Lavinia, it was not a happy one at all.

'They're a bribe,' said Lavinia. She looked cross. Everything makes Lavinia cross. 'My stupid father's decided to marry his secretary. He says so in his letter. I shall have to go and spend Christmas with them both. Ugh!'

'Perhaps she's nice,' I said.

'She's foul,' said Lavinia. 'I hated her when she was just his secretary and I hate her even more now.'

'Well, we have to spend Christmas in *Cambridge* with my *brother*,' said Daisy. 'Ugh!'

I think she was trying to be helpful, but Christmas in Cambridge sounded quite lovely, and Bertie, Daisy's brother, is very nice indeed.

'Poor Beanie has to spend Christmas with *my* horrid family,' said Kitty, hugging me. 'Two weeks of Binny – imagine!'

'Where are your parents going?' asked Daisy, staring at me.

'To Spain,' I said. 'On holiday.'

'And mine are in Hong Kong!' said Hazel. 'Think of that!'

'I wish my father was in Hong Kong too,' said Lavinia, and that was the end of that. But Hazel squeezed my hand when no one else was looking. Hazel is very clever. She understands everything.

I am now in Kitty and Binny's big white house in a place called Belgravia, which is in London. It is part of a long row of houses the colour of cream lace, which stare out onto a square of trees and grass, and then more white houses beyond that. It has three floors and a basement, which is where the kitchens are, and a garden behind it with a shed and lots of trees. One of them is blooming, even though it is almost Christmas. I thought this was because London has strange weather, but the Freebodys' maid, Louise, says that it is the sort of tree that flowers in winter. Behind the garden is a lane, and behind that are more gardens and houses. London does go on and on.

When we arrived at Paddington Station, we were met by Kitty's father, Mr Freebody. I thought Mr Freebody's car would get stuck in a snow drift, but I think perhaps he was driving too fast, and simply went through all the drifts. Mr Freebody drives very fast, and also does not put the top of his car up. Kitty and Binny squealed with delight all the way home, but it made me worry. We drove up to the big black front door of the house, and there were boys in raggedy jackets and big shoes playing in the street. They threw balls of snow at us. Some of them splattered across the windows of Mr Freebody's car, and some of them burst against Mr Freebody's head. Mr Freebody roared with laughter and swerved the car, and the boys had to jump out of the way. I was afraid they would be hurt, but they were all right. Louise told us that they were rough boys from a few streets away, who liked to cause trouble.

'They'll end up in gaol,' she said, shaking her head. That made me worry too, because gaol is not a nice place. Louise is interested in crime, a bit like Daisy's maid, Hetty, though she is older and taller, a proper grown-up, with mousy flat hair under her cap.

At this moment Louise is upstairs unpacking our things, and Binny is downstairs being told off not very seriously by Mrs Freebody (Mrs Freebody is very pretty, like Kitty, and laughs a lot, like Binny), because she pulled the cat's tail, and also because of that old lady on the train. Mrs Freebody is explaining what poverty is, and why it is important not to pretend to be poor, and Binny is saying that she *knows* how dreadful poverty is, and that is why she wanted to save her allowance but have the chocolate as well. Now Mrs Freebody is kissing Binny all over her face and Binny is squealing and Mrs Freebody is saying, 'You horror, you little horror, why must you always make trouble? You know I can't get on without you.'

She is saying that because Binny did slightly almost die last term during the Bonfire Night Murder Case – but so did we all. It wasn't very nice.

I am a little bit shocked about Binny and the chocolate. I also know how dreadful poverty is, because it happened to Daddy when he was the age I am now. He had to sleep in one bed with all three of his brothers, and he had to black shoes to pay for his school uniform. But then he decided to stop paying for school uniforms and went to work in a pin factory instead, and he did it so well that now he owns that factory and five others. That is why I don't have to pay for my own school uniform or shine shoes. Sometimes I wish we *were* poor, so that I wouldn't be made to go to school, where I can never understand the books we read or the sums we are made to write. Even so, I still know that what Binny did was wrong.

I am not sure I should have told that story about Daddy. Kitty, please don't put that in the finished story.

I am now in Mr Freebody's study, and it feels like a strange place to be. There are books everywhere, and a big wooden desk with a fat chair behind it which I am sitting in. On the desk is a big metal machine with buttons and a trumpety thing at one end. Kitty brought me in here twenty minutes ago and pointed to it and said, 'There.'

'What is it?' I asked.

'It's Dad's,' said Kitty. 'It's a Dictaphone. It's for recording what you say, so someone else can listen to it later and type it up.'

I still didn't understand. Sometimes I think everyone else in the world sees and hears things properly, while

233

they fly straight past my brain and out of the nearest window.

'It's for *you*, Beans,' said Kitty, sighing. 'You can use it this hols. I know you think you're no good at writing, but you're good at *telling* me stories when no one else is about, so I thought you might like it. I can type your story out for you afterwards. I've got Dad to agree not to come in here while you're talking – he's on his own hols from his company now – so the only person you've got to worry about is Binny. Just ignore her like you would Tibbles the cat and she'll go away.'

Kitty is my absolutely best friend, and this is why. I am using the Dictaphone so that I have a record of this holiday, which I want to do because this will be a good hols. I am with Kitty, and it is nearly Christmas, and I am going to be brave and not mind that Daddy has taken Mummy to Spain without me, because they want to see whether the sun makes her better again. That does not matter at all.

II
Later

I am in Mr Freebody's study again. It is dark and the lamps are lit, but the snow has stopped falling. There was a story on the wireless about a convict who escaped from Holloway Prison. Binny said, 'OOH!' and I must have squeaked because Kitty rolled her eyes and told me that Holloway is far away, in the north-east of London.

'The east is where all the criminals live,' said Binny, her voice gaspy. 'Louise was telling me. It's lawless and awful, and did you know there was a little boy who killed his—'

'ROBERTA,' said Mr Freebody, which is Binny's real name. 'ENOUGH. Darling, could you please speak to Louise about her colourful imagination? I don't like her putting ideas like this into the girls' heads. They've only been back a few hours.'

'I doubt it was Louise who began the conversation,' said Mrs Freebody, rolling her eyes the way Kitty does. 'Binny, sit DOWN and stop stabbing your carrots like that. Look at how Kitty is eating hers.'

'*Look* at Kitty,' muttered Binny into her plate. '*Perfect* Kitty.'

Kitty pinched Binny under the table like a crab. Binny howled, and was sent up to her room by Mr Freebody.

Kitty told me it was nonsense, but somehow Binny's story was still frightening me when we went up to our room after dinner. I stood and stared out of the front window while Kitty was brushing her hair. The snow looked like a photograph with the lamps lighting it. And there on the pavement was a set of black footprints. They went from the right to the left and stopped at the door of our house. I thought about what Hazel would say if she was here. Everyone had been in the house for hours. Who else could it be? Was it one of the naughty boys, about to play a trick? Or . . . someone worse?

'Kitty!' I cried. 'Kitty!' I pointed out of the window.

'Oh, Beans, don't listen to Binny!' said Kitty. 'She talks stupid nonsense. That's the *postman* – didn't you hear the letterbox rattle five minutes ago?'

I shook my head, and felt stupid and very little.

'IT'S FOR ME!' screamed Binny, who had got out of her room and was now downstairs. 'A PARCEL WITH MY NAME ON IT!'

I heard Louise and Mrs Freebody trying to shush her, Mrs Freebody not very seriously, and what sounded like Binny climbing onto a table. Something shattered.

'Come here, Beans, and let me plait your hair,' said Kitty sharply. She plaited it, and it pulled. I tried not to let my eyes water. But something was worrying me. It was not until just now that I realized what it was: there were no footprints leading *away* again.

III
23rd December

Binny did not come out for breakfast this morning, even though the Freebodys' cook, Mrs Summerscale, makes a very nice one. She stayed in her room, playing with the present she was sent yesterday evening. I think Kitty is jealous.

'Opening her presents early!' she said. 'It isn't fair, I'm not allowed to!'

This made me realize that I don't know what I want as a present. I want Kitty to get the new hair curlers she has been staring at in a magazine for months. I made her some from rags, but they are not quite the same. I want Lavinia to get a new doll, because her old one is quite battered. (She keeps it in her trunk, and thinks no one knows about it.) I want Daisy to get a detective kit (although I know that is taken care of, because Hazel has made her one), and I want Hazel to have new notebooks (although I know that Daisy has got her some). Before last term I wanted Kitty and Lavinia and me to be proper Detective Society members – but last term we became part of the Bonfire Night Murder. I didn't like *how* that happened – I was so afraid, down in the tunnel, when I thought Kitty might die and that was why I knew I had to be brave and save her because I could not bear that – but we *are* detectives now. Daisy even said we can have badges.

So what do I want? I want silly things. I want Mummy to be well again, and for her and Daddy to come home to collect me. I want to ride Boggles, my pony, down the lane next to our house. I want Hazel and Daisy and Lavinia to be here as well, but of course that is impossible because Hazel and Daisy are in Cambridge, and Lavinia has gone to her father's house in Leamington Spa. I do miss them quite a bit.

IV

Kitty just came in and found me crying. She said I was a fool to get so upset talking to a silly Dictaphone machine, and hugged me.

Then we heard shouting downstairs. It was Mrs Summerscale, the cook. Although she makes very nice food, Mrs Summerscale is quite a cross person, a bit like Lavinia.

'That girl has stolen the trifle!' she was shouting.

By *that girl* she meant Binny. Mrs Summerscale went rushing up the stairs to pound on Binny's bedroom door, and then Mrs Freebody joined her, laughing, and Binny screamed at them to go away. Kitty went outside to watch and dragged me with her.

Finally Binny opened her door, looking cross.

'What do you want?' she asked.

'You ate my trifle!' shouted Mrs Summerscale. 'A great scoop out of the side of it! If you wanted breakfast, you should have asked! That was for your dinner later!'

'I never ate anything!' said Binny. 'I'm playing with my new doll, I tell you! I haven't been out of my room.

Someone else must have eaten it, for it wasn't me! And anyway, I hate trifle. It's ugh.'

I looked at Kitty. Her face was scrunched up thinkingly. 'Do you believe her?' I asked.

'Well,' said Kitty. 'You know, I do. Binny *does* hate trifle. It's always just Dad and me who eat it. So who did it, if she didn't? Beanie, do you think this might be *a mystery*?'

I felt thrilled inside. 'If we detected it, Daisy and Hazel would be so proud!' I said. I thought about that. 'Well, Hazel would be proud.'

'Yes, it would be one in the eye for Daisy!' said Kitty, grinning. 'Beans, let's do it! If there's a mystery, we must solve it! We are proper Detective Society members now, after all.'

We came back into this study, and Kitty made a list while I looked at it.

I wasn't sure it was as good as one of Hazel and Daisy's lists, but at least it looked pretty in Kitty's handwriting.

THE TRIFLE THIEF: SUSPECTS

- Binny (she denies it, and she hates trifle)
- Mrs Summerscale (but she made it)
- Louise (could it be her?)
- ~~Mum~~ Mrs Freebody (Mum is like Binny, she hates trifle)
- ~~Dad~~ Mr Freebody (but he went out straight after breakfast, and we saw him eat three rashers of bacon and two fried eggs and toast so he could not be hungry)

- The bad boys
- Us (but it wasn't us)

I tried to make Kitty put in the person who made the footprints in the snow, but she told me not to be silly, those were from the postman. She said it with her eyes rolling so I knew I wasn't allowed to tell her I was worried What if those prints *were* from someone else? Why had they not gone away from our house again? What if it *was* the convict? What if the convict was hiding somewhere nearby? Did convicts like trifle?

I am worried that convicts may like trifle.

V

Kitty and I have been investigating. First we went to look at Binny, to rule her out for good by making sure there was no trifle on her clothes. Binny is quite dirty and always gets her clothes smeary with food so this was a good idea of Kitty's. Kitty saw a stain on Binny's sleeve and tried to hold her down and investigate her, but Binny bit Kitty and ran away. So we don't know if it was a trifle stain, and we still cannot rule her out for good.

Then we went to look for Louise. We found her tidying Mrs Freebody's room.

'Hello, girls!' she said, standing up with a pile of Mrs Freebody's scarves in her arms.

'Hello, Louise!' said Kitty cheerfully. 'Do you like trifle?'

I was looking at Louise, and I am sure she blushed! Daisy would say that this was suspicious behaviour, I knew.

'No!' she said, and turned away to Mrs Freebody's chest of drawers. She was folding things very neatly and carefully. 'Trifle is bad for my digestion. I never eat sweets.'

Then we went down to talk to Mrs Summerscale. The kitchens are all the way down in the basement, except this basement has a little window at the front that looks up at the street outside, and another one that looks up at the garden. The window to the street was all dark with snow, but the window to the garden was clean, as if the snow had all been knocked away, and a little bit open. I wondered if I had seen a clue.

Mrs Summerscale was marching around the room looking into cupboards and opening the door of the lit range. She was behaving as though she had lost something. When she saw us, her eyes narrowed.

'I can't find the tin of gingerbread!' she said. 'Have you taken it?'

'Of course not!' said Kitty, crossing her arms. 'Do you mean . . . it's gone too?'

'That is exactly what I'm implying,' snapped Mrs Summerscale. 'We have a thief in this house! Which means no bunbreak for you three today. Nor tomorrow neither! I was going to make mince pies, but with a thief in the house, I don't think I shall. I saw your sister running away earlier, holding that new toy of hers – no one can do a thing with her. Your mother's too lax with you both!'

'Is it true that Louise doesn't like sweets?' I asked. I wanted to rule out Louise.

Mrs Summerscale snorted. 'Of course she does,' she said. 'She's just being faddy. I've seen her in here, taking little bits from the sides of things when she thinks I don't notice. But stealing a whole tin, or a great chunk of trifle – that's not Louise's way. She's too tidy. No, I think the culprit this time is *much* younger.'

She glared at us both until Kitty nudged me and pulled me out of the kitchen.

I had noticed earlier that Louise was tidy. I felt proud that I had seen a clue. But could we be sure? I knew that Daisy would say that we had not found *concrete proof* to rule Louise out yet.

Investigating crimes is confusing.

But one thing we know is that there really *is* a mystery. Food is going missing. And now that a tin of gingerbread has gone missing too, I have an idea of what we could call it: the Mystery of the Missing Bunbreak.

VI
Afternoon

Perhaps *missing bunbreak* is not strictly accurate any more, for half a braised ham has gone missing now. It was to be tea tonight. Binny has locked herself in her room. Mrs Freebody has stopped laughing about the thefts, and has become very nearly serious. I think it is because Mr Freebody has come home and is unhappy about the ham.

I am talking into the Dictaphone while the rough boys are running about outside again, throwing snowballs at each other and singing rude carols. I tried to see if any of them looked particularly full just now, but I couldn't tell. Earlier I told Kitty about the clean back window I had seen when we were talking to Mrs Summerscale in the kitchen. 'What if one of the boys broke in?' I asked.

'Interesting theory, Detective Beanie!' said Kitty. She looked pleased. 'Let us go and look!'

We crept down the stairs and let ourselves out into the garden by the little back door above the kitchens. Kitty's garden has a wall around it, covered in creepers, and a sweet little shed in the back corner which the vines have almost covered as well. The window into the kitchen is on the opposite side of the garden from the shed. I think those are detective observations.

Kitty and I went to kneel in front of the kitchen window, to see if we could find any new clues. It had certainly been opened recently, for all the snow had been wiped away from it by someone's hand. It opened inwards, and it looked as though Mrs Summerscale or Louise had forgotten to latch it. Kitty pushed at it.

'Are you going to climb in?' I asked.

'Er, not likely,' said Kitty. 'It's *dirty*, Beans. This coat is practically new!'

I didn't want to either, in case I fell. But I looked at the space, and knew that Kitty or I could get through easily. So could one of the boys – and so could an adult, if they were quite thin. Were convicts thin?

Then I heard something behind us. I turned round. The door to the shed was hanging slightly open.

'Was it like that before?' whispered Kitty, turning too. 'Oh, say it was. Wasn't it?'

I couldn't remember. I am a bad detective. But I thought that it might not have been. I reached for Kitty's hand, and she squeezed it.

'I'll give you five shillings if you go and look inside,' said Kitty. 'Ten shillings. *A guinea.* I can't go, I shall die.'

I told myself that if I went and looked, Mummy would be better. If I looked, she and Daddy would come home, and everything I wanted for everyone's Christmases would come true. If I went and looked, I could prove that I was being a goose about the convict.

I took a step forward, and then another, and another. My hand went up and I pushed the door open. It was dark inside and smelled dirty. It was a familiar smell, and I thought it smelled like boys when they don't wash. I gasped, and Kitty must have thought that I had seen something. She screamed, and I jumped, and the door opened all the way.

There was no one inside. It was empty. But there was a blanket in the far corner, and on it was a tin, all covered in dark crumbs.

We had found the missing gingerbread.

'What are you girls doing?' Mrs Freebody shouted, sticking her head out of a window above us. 'Are you playing a game?'

Kitty thought very fast and shouted back that we were playing What's the Time, Mr Wolf? and then Mrs Freebody looked excited and said that we should have a games evening. So we had to come in and stop investigating – and I am glad. My heart is still pounding now.

VII
Evening

I am recording this very quietly because I am worried. Kitty doesn't believe me but I am *sure* that there is someone in the house with us. I keep looking around at the books on the walls of this study and thinking that the candlelight making them flicker is someone in a corner.

The Freebodys' games are not the sort of games Mummy and Daddy and I play. They all happen in the dark, with fire. We played Blind Man's Buff, and Wink Murder (I was the murderer, and I cried, and Kitty said *Beans!* I hate disappointing her, but I do hate murder), and then Snap Dragon. Mrs Freebody brought out a plate of raisins soaked in brandy and lit them, so they burned and turned blue. You are supposed to catch them straight out of the bowl and eat them. Binny ate twenty. I ate the one that Kitty gave me.

Mr and Mrs Freebody laughed and teased each other, and Binny and Kitty, and I tried so hard to be brave and not mind about Mummy and Daddy.

The last game of the evening was Shadow Buff. One person sits in front of a sheet with a candle behind it, and all the others stand between the sheet and the candle with silly disguises on, and cast the maddest shadows they can manage. I saw a horse, and a monster with wild hair, and an old man, and Cleopatra, and Sherlock Holmes.

'So, who were we?' asked Kitty at the end. I said that Kitty was Sherlock, and Mrs Freebody was Cleopatra, and Binny was the old man, and Mr Freebody was the horse, and Louise was the monster.

'WRONG!' screamed Binny. '*I* was the *monster*! And what old man? There wasn't one. Louise didn't play, silly – she hates games like this!'

I got the shivers all over. I had seen five shadows. 'What's up?' asked Kitty, but my teeth were chattering. *Who had been the old man?* The room was all dark. *Anyone* might have crept up and . . .

That is why I am sure that someone is here with us. The Mystery of the Missing Bunbreak is not at all fun any more.

VIII
Christmas Eve

I was very glad to wake up this morning. Then I heard Louise outside our room. 'This mud!' she was saying. 'All over the clean sheets, after I folded them so neatly! Binny Freebody, have you been tracking mud into the house?'

'Why does everyone always blame me?' Binny shrieked from her room.

'WHO TOOK THE KIPPERS FOR BREAK-FAST?' screamed Mrs Summerscale downstairs.

I threw the covers back over my head and wished that I was anywhere else.

Kitty came and sat on my bed. 'Do you think it *is* Binny?' she whispered. 'Is she playing an enormous prank? Or *is* it those boys? They came carolling a few nights ago, Mum says, and Mrs Summerscale sent them away. They hate her now. It can't be Louise, can it?' I shook my head, because it wasn't logical that tidy Louise would ruin the sheets, or hide a tin of gingerbread in a shed. 'Or – Beans, what if it really is . . . THE CONVICT? They still haven't caught him.'

I shrieked. I couldn't help it. 'You're awful,' I said to Kitty.

'I'm only saying!' she said. 'It might be! Oh, come on, Beans, we could outwit a silly convict!'

'He'd be bigger than us,' I said, thinking about the footprints again and shuddering. 'I don't like it, Kitty! I don't like this mystery!'

'We'd be cleverer than him, though!' said Kitty. 'If it *is* him, I mean. It might not be! I still think Binny's acting very oddly. Come on, let's get dressed. It's breakfast time!'

'Breakfast with no kippers,' I reminded her.

'Who likes kippers?' asked Kitty. 'Apart from Daisy, of course.'

'I miss the others,' I said, before I could stop myself. 'Daisy and Hazel and Lavinia.'

'I know,' said Kitty, and she put her arms around me. 'And you miss your parents too. I can tell. You know, Beans, you're an awfully brave person.'

248

IX
Later

After breakfast Mr Freebody went out. He said he had some last-minute work to do, and we believed him, but then he came back half an hour later, roaring with laughter and dragging an enormous tree behind him. Helping him were the rough boys. I gasped, and went to stand behind the sofa in case they did something awful. But the boys seemed quite cheerful. I saw that they had shillings stuffed into their pockets, and buns in their hands – Mr Freebody must have paid them off. They also did not look angry any more, or hungry – and they took off their dirty shoes at the door. Were they really suspects?

I had an idea. I went up to one of them and sniffed him. He smelled a little like a boy who had not washed, but all the same it was not the smell I had smelled in the shed yesterday. Kitty looked at me oddly, but I thought I had done well. From the boys' behaviour, and the way they looked and smelled, I thought we could rule them out.

The boys put up the Christmas tree, and then clattered back into the street. I made sure that the same number went out as had come in, and I could see Kitty counting too. Then I felt shuddery, because we were ruling everyone out apart from the one person I didn't want it to be.

Kitty began to drape the tree in cotton wool, and hang it with baubles, but Binny did not help. She was in the corner, playing with something. 'Binny, what is that?' snapped Kitty at last. 'Ugh, it's filthy! Where did you get it?'

'It's my new doll!' said Binny. 'It was in the parcel I got just after we came home. Remember?'

I looked at the doll in her arms. And then I had the sort of moment that Daisy and Hazel are always having, and I thought I never should. It made me realize that being a detective might not be about being the cleverest and most noticing person in the world. It's just about knowing things. And I knew that doll.

'Binny,' I said. 'Was the parcel for you?'

'Course it was,' she said. 'It had my name on it.'

'Did it say Roberta? Or Binny?'

'Binny, *obviously*,' said Binny. 'It was all smudged, but I could read it.'

My heart was beating very hard. 'Kitty!' I said. 'Come upstairs. *Now*.'

'What's up, Beans?' asked Kitty. My knees were all wobbly, but I ran up the stairs.

'The parcel didn't say Binny,' I told her. 'It said *Beanie*.'

'That's silly,' said Kitty. 'Who knows you're here and would send you a parcel and not me one as well, and call you Beanie and not Rebecca? Your parents call you Rebecca, don't they?'

'Only one person would!' I said. 'I think I know what's been happening, Kitty! The doll wasn't a *present*. It was supposed to be a message.'

'From *who*?' said Kitty. I could tell I was making her cross. It was not a nice thing to do, but I didn't have time to explain. I marched up the stairs, feeling like there was a quite different Rebecca Martineau coming from inside me. Then I stopped outside the airing cupboard, the one that had made Louise upset with its dirty sheets, and pulled it open with a hand that only shook a little. There was a small part of me that thought I *could* be wrong after all, and I did not like the idea of opening the door to a convict.

But I wasn't wrong. I pushed aside some sheets.

'Oi!' said the person behind them.

'OH!' said Kitty. 'Oh, BEANIE!'

'There!' I said. 'Look! It's Lavinia.'

X
Evening

I was called away to dinner just then, but now I am back, and can finish the story. Lavinia was very grubby, and she smelled horrible, the exact smell from the shed. Her coat was covered with the remains of the ham and the kippers and the trifle, and there were dark bags under her eyes.

Kitty shouted and almost hugged her, and then pushed her away and said, 'HOW did you get here? HOW?'

'Took the train,' said Lavinia. 'Came to find you. Left a message for you, Beanie, but you didn't get it. Like an idiot, I thought I'd wait out in the shed and scrounge from the kitchen until you understood my message and let me in. I couldn't just ring the front doorbell in case Kitty's parents saw me and sent me away. But, Lord, it's cold! I really thought I'd die. I finally decided to slip into the house and stay there last night, while you were running about in the garden. Thought it would be funny to give Beans a scare while you were playing games, so I did, and then I came back up to hide here.'

'But WHY?' shouted Kitty.

'Didn't want to spend Christmas with Dad and his awful *fiancee*,' said Lavinia, scowling. 'I *told* you. It wasn't fair – my brothers were well out of it. Giles is in the army now, and Julian's in America. They're trying to get as far as they can from Dad, so I didn't see why I shouldn't as well.'

'Why didn't you just ask to come and spend Christmas with us?' asked Kitty. 'We've got rooms and rooms, you prize idiot!'

'You might have said no,' said Lavinia, looking down. 'I know you like each other best, just like Daisy and Hazel do. It's never me that people want around.'

'Of course it is!' I cried, and I hugged her, even though she smelled awful. 'I like you! And I knew it was you when I saw that doll. You keep her in your trunk. I knew you were trying to tell me you were here.'

Lavinia hugged me back, very tightly, and that was when Mrs Freebody came up the stairs and saw the three of us.

She shrieked, then she made Lavinia have three baths and have her clothes burnt, and she put her into one of Kitty's old dresses, and brushed her hair into ringlets. Lavinia grumbled, but Kitty and I think she rather enjoyed it. Then she was brought downstairs and we watched as she ate a tray of mince pies and a side of beef. Mrs Summerscale was furious, and did not want to let Lavinia have it, until she made a grumbling noise through a mince pie. 'Your food is good,' she said to Mrs Summerscale. 'Thanks and all.'

Mrs Summerscale's frown shrank, and then she said, 'Well. I suppose, if you're hungry.'

Lavinia told me and Kitty later exactly what had happened. She had sneaked off the train home to Leamington Spa while it waited on the station without Matron seeing – by getting on one side of it and then off on the other. Then she smudged her ticket's destination and used it to get on another train to London. Then she took a bus to Kitty's house. She arrived that first evening, walked up to the front door and left the parcel with the doll in it for me. She covered her tracks by walking away backwards (this is why I only saw the footsteps up to the door. Lavinia says it seemed like a detective-y thing to do. Kitty says it was a stupid thing to do), and then waited for me. When I did not come to the door, she went round towards the garden side of the house and climbed the wall. She slept in the shed that night, and then began stealing food from the house the next morning, when she found the kitchen window open. When we came out to investigate the garden, she ran in through the back door – she says she was cross with us for not understanding she was there, and wanted to trick us, which is a very Lavinia thing to say and do.

Mr and Mrs Freebody are so nice and jolly that they have forgiven Lavinia, though I think they are rather worried about being accused of kidnapping. They have telephoned Deepdean, who have telephoned Lavinia's father, and Lavinia will have to go home again – though not until after Christmas.

We also tried to telephone St Lucy's College, where Daisy and Hazel are staying, to tell them about Lavinia – but we were told that Daisy and Hazel were not available. Something seems to be going on in Cambridge – 'As usual!' said Kitty. 'Those two, honestly!'

I do miss Daisy and Hazel, but all the same I think I would rather be here with Kitty and Lavinia. It sounds as though Daisy and Hazel may be facing a mystery even more alarming than ours.

We gathered round the tree for carols after dinner, and to listen to the wireless – and we heard in a news bulletin that the convict has been caught and sent back to prison. All that time he was really in Wapping, which Kitty says is not near us at all. So I was silly to be afraid.

Then there was another telephone call – for me. It was very wavery and far away, but it was my daddy's voice. He told me that Mummy is doing well, much better, and that they have decided to come home in a few days' time to see me. Christmas is tomorrow, and Kitty wants me to hurry up and go to sleep so that Father Christmas can bring us our presents, but it feels to me as though Christmas is already here.

afraid.

Then there was

was very wavery an

voice. He told me

beast, and that the

few days time to se

King wants me to ha

Christmas can begin

as though Christmas

THE GREAT DETECTIVE QUIZ

And finally, detectives, it's time to see how much attention you've been paying to my books! Here's a fiendish quiz about Hazel and Daisy's adventures. See how many you can get right – the answers are at the back of this book!

Murder Most Unladylike

1. What is Daisy's nickname for Hazel?
2. What is Beanie's proper full name?
3. What nickname do the Deepdean girls give Miss Griffin's box of confiscated possessions?
4. What emblem is painted in the middle of Kitty's Ouija board?
5. Which medicine do Daisy and Hazel take to make themselves throw up?

w Labrador

r talking in

n make for

)ctor?
me of Hide
birthday?
   Daisy and

oress's gold
way, where

siness?
id the neck

zel pretend
e trying to

b Witch

)so's magic

17. Which country is the Orient Express passing through when the crime is committed?
18. What is Hazel's Chinese name?

Jolly Foul Play

19. What is the name of Beanie's pet dormouse?
20. What does Florence Hamersley hope to compete in at the Olympics?
21. Name the twins who live in Clementine's dorm and have rhyming names?
22. Who is the new headmistress at Deepdean?
23. What do Alexander and Hazel use to keep their letters to each other secret?
24. How do Daisy and Hazel listen in on the Five's conversation in their dorm?

Mistletoe and Murder

25. What is the name of the secret society that Daisy and Hazel unearth in Cambridge?
26. Where do Hazel, Daisy, Alex and George find the best Chelsea buns?
27. Whose room do Hazel and Daisy stay in at St Lucy's?
28. What does Amanda call her bike, which confuses Hazel the first time she hears it?

29. Which bookshop do Hazel and Daisy visit in Cambridge?

30. What is on the Christmas card that Daisy gives to George and Alexander?

ANSWERS

Codebreaking with Hazel Wong

Reversing words
  deepdean school for girls

Pig Latin
  now you can all speak Pig Latin!

Morse code
  A -- / · · - / · - · / - · · / · / · - · / = murder
  B -- / - · - - / · · · / - / · / · - · / - · - -/ = mystery
  C · - · / · / - · · // · · · · / · / · - · / · - · / · · / - · /
    -- · / = red herring

  detective = - · · / · / - / · / - · · · / - / · · / · · · - / ·
  arsenic = · - / · - · / · · · / · / - · / · · / - · - ·
  Hazel = · · · · / · - / -- · · / · / · - · ·
  Daisy = - · · / · - / · · / · · · / - · --

Caesar shift cipher
  FUXPSHWV = crumpets
  IRRWSULQWV = footprints
  FOXHV = clues

The cipher with a left shift of three:
Normal:

A	B	C	D	E	F	G	H	I	J	K	L	M	N	O	P	Q	R	S	T	U	V	W	X	Y	Z

Cipher:

X	Y	Z	A	B	C	D	E	F	G	H	I	J	K	L	M	N	O	P	Q	R	S	T	U	V	W

Zntavslvat Tynff = magnifying glass (left shift of thirteen)
Mbylfiwe Birgym = Sherlock Holmes (right shift of six)
Paroay Igkygx = Julius Caesar (left shift of six)

Transposition cipher
FIRST CLASS MURDER

Letter to Daisy
Dear Daisy

I am writing you a letter in code, so that you can practise your codebreaking. And this time you mustn't give up before you get to the end, because I have something very important to tell you. I had a telephone call today. You tried to listen in (I saw you at Matron's office door). I know you didn't hear properly, because you've been trying to ask me questions about it ever since. It was from my father (you guessed that) and it was about my grandfather (I'm sure you guessed that too). He has been ill, and he has died, and that is not a secret or a mystery. But now my father wants me to come home to mourn him – and, Daisy, he says you should come with me, so I won't be alone on the journey. I know Hong Kong isn't what you are used to, but I have met your family, and now I want you to meet mine.

Say you will?

Hazel

The Great Detective Quiz

Murder Most Unladylike

1. What is Daisy's nickname for Hazel?
   Watson
2. What is Beanie's proper full name?
   Rebecca Martineau
3. What nickname do the Deepdean girls give Miss Griffin's box of confiscated possessions?
   Davey Jones
4. What emblem is painted in the middle of Kitty's Ouija board?
   A yellow eye
5. Which medicine do Daisy and Hazel take to make themselves throw up?
   Ipecac

Arsenic for Tea

6. What is the name of the fat old yellow Labrador at the Wellses' house, Fallingford?
   Toast Dog
7. Who do Daisy and Hazel overhear talking in the maze?
   Uncle Felix and Mr Curtis

266

8. What type of cake does Chapman make for Daisy's birthday tea?

   A chocolate cake, oozing cream

9. What is the name of the Wellses' doctor?

   Doctor Cooper

10. Who is chosen to count in the game of Hide and Seek at Fallingford for Daisy's birthday?

    Beanie

11. What does the inspector send to Daisy and Hazel at the end of the case?

    Shiny silver badges saying 'DETECTIVE'

First Class Murder

12. Exactly what does the Orient Express's gold plaque say? Or, to put this another way, where is it going?

    Calais – Simplon – Istanbul

13. What is the name of Mr Daunt's business?

    Daunt's Diet Pills

14. What gemstone is stolen from around the neck of Mrs Daunt?

    A ruby, surrounded with diamonds

15. What activity book do Daisy and Hazel pretend to work on together while they are trying to solve the case?

    The Baffle Book

16. What does Hazel find in Il Mysterioso's magic box?
    Forged birth certificates
17. Which country is the Orient Express passing through when the crime is committed?
    Jugo-Slavia
18. What is Hazel's Chinese name?
    Wong Fung Ying

Jolly Foul Play

19. What is the name of Beanie's pet dormouse?
    Chutney
20. What does Florence Hamersley hope to compete in at the Olympics?
    Hurdles
21. Name the twins who live in Clementine's dorm and have rhyming names?
    Rose and Jose Pritchett
22. Who is the new headmistress at Deepdean?
    Miss Barnard
23. What do Alexander and Hazel use to keep their letters to each other secret?
    Invisible ink
24. How do Daisy and Hazel listen in on the Five's conversation in their dorm?
    They climb onto the roof of House

Mistletoe and Murder

25. What is the name of the secret society that Daisy and Hazel unearth in Cambridge?
    The Night Climbers

26. Where do Hazel, Daisy, Alex and George find the best Chelsea buns?
    Fitzbillies Tea Rooms

27. Whose room do Hazel and Daisy stay in at St Lucy's?
    King Henry's

28. What does Amanda call her bike, which confuses Hazel the first time she hears it?
    The Horse

29. Which bookshop do Hazel and Daisy visit in Cambridge?
    Heffers

30. What is on the Christmas card that Daisy gives to George and Alexander?
    Cats with a Christmas cracker

Acknowledgments

This has been an enormously fun book to work on! I hope you've enjoyed it as much as I did.

As I said in my dedication, if you love Daisy and Hazel, and if you have stuck with them through the series, no matter where or who you are, this book is for you. You deserve it! Thank you.

I'd also like to thank my agent, Gemma Cooper, and my editor, Natalie Doherty, for making this book possible. And huge thanks to the whole team at Puffin, especially Tom Rawlinson, for working so hard on it!

Finally, thanks to the Ladies for their invaluable advice on Hong Kong bunbreak. We got there in the end!

Read all the books in the
Murder Most Unladylike
series . . .

sing Tie?
ystery?

ered on
ing.
r, but